Suddenly she was hyperaware of how alone they were. Just the two of them. With nothing but the night around them.

"Whoever is trying to kill you won't know you're no longer working for PPS. And they might not care even if they do."

"What are you saying? That I should run off to L.A., where I'll be safe?" Cassie hadn't realized it, but she'd been counting on Mike to back her up, to agree that staying and working with the team was the best course.

"No. It might be selfishness on my part, but I want you to stay."

Cassie let out the breath she'd been holding. Mike wanting her in Colorado, especially for selfish reasons, meant more than she could say. Since that morning when she'd lost her hearing, she'd dreamed of finding a man who would treat her as a partner. A man who believed she was his equal. "I guess I need to figure out where I'm going to stay."

"I have an idea. And since my original assignment with PPS is over, I might be in the market for something new."

"Or something old, like protecting me?"

"I have the feeling protecting you will never get old."

ANN VOSS PETERSON

SPECIAL ASSIGNMENT

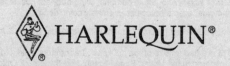

HARLEQUIN®

TORONTO • NEW YORK • LONDON
AMSTERDAM • PARIS • SYDNEY • HAMBURG
STOCKHOLM • ATHENS • TOKYO • MILAN • MADRID
PRAGUE • WARSAW • BUDAPEST • AUCKLAND

To Denise Zaza and Allison Lyons. Thanks for
inviting me to contribute to this fun series!

Special thanks and acknowledgment to
Ann Voss Peterson for her contribution to the
BODYGUARDS UNLIMITED, DENVER, CO miniseries.

ISBN-13: 978-0-373-88755-2
ISBN-10:   0-373-88755-8

SPECIAL ASSIGNMENT

ABOUT THE AUTHOR

Ever since she was a little girl making her own books out of construction paper, Ann Voss Peterson wanted to write. So when it came time to choose a major at the University of Wisconsin, creative writing was her only choice. Of course, writing wasn't a *practical* choice—one needs to earn a living. So Ann found various jobs, including proofreading legal transcripts, working with quarter horses and washing windows. But no matter how she earned her paycheck, she continued to write the type of stories that captured her heart and imagination—romantic suspense. Ann lives near Madison, Wisconsin, with her husband, her two young sons, her border collie and her quarter horse mare. Ann loves to hear from readers. E-mail her at ann@annvosspeterson.com or visit her Web site at www.annvosspeterson.com.

Books by Ann Voss Peterson

CAST OF CHARACTERS

Detective Mike Lawson—Mike bleeds blue. A cop from a long line of cops, confronted with widespread corruption tainting his beloved Denver PD. Choosing personal ethics over loyalty, now he has to pay....

Cassie Allen—An overachiever all her life, Cassie was a computer whiz and an accomplished classical pianist before she graduated from high school. But after losing her hearing, Cassie set out to prove she is just like anyone else.

Evangeline Prescott—Evangeline likes to give Prescott Personal Security employees the opportunity to prove themselves. But when Cassie's life is threatened, Evangeline pulls out the stops to make sure she's safe.

The Dirty Three—Trio of Denver PD officers arrested for stealing from drug dealers. Now they want revenge.

Deputy Chief Wade Lawson—Mike's father can't forgive his son.

Detective Tim Grady—Mike's partner is the only cop he can trust.

Milo Kardascian—The CEO has an old grudge against Mike.

James Durgin—Is the millionaire afraid for his life or playing tricks?

Chapter One

No amount of booze could wipe a conscience clean. Not that Mike Lawson hadn't given it one hell of a shot tonight.

He concentrated on putting one foot in front of the other, stumbling in the direction of the fleabag motel next door to the Beer-ly Alive Tavern. Gravel crunched and scuffed under his boots, the sound brittle as breaking glass in the cool April night. Not that he could feel the temperature. His nose and lips were numb as a plastic mask.

He groped in his pocket and pulled out a room key on one of those old-fashioned plastic paddles. No key cards at this place. At least he had brains enough to check into a room before bellying up to attempt to suck the worm out of a bottle of mescal. He sure as hell didn't need to risk driving back to the ranch. As a cop,

Mike had seen what happened when booze and cars mixed. He didn't need to add vehicular manslaughter to his list of sins. That list was long enough already.

"God, I was hoping you'd climb behind the wheel, Lawson." A voice ground out from the shadows. The light from a nearby post gleamed off a shaved scalp. "I'd love to watch the boys slap the cuffs on you and jam an intoximeter tube down your throat."

Even in his inebriated state, Mike recognized the voice. His ears started to pound. "Aren't you in prison yet, Fisher?" He tried to hold his head steady and squinted into the shadows.

Three men stood next to his pickup truck. Fisher, Stevens and Rodriguez. The Curly, Larry and Moe of the Denver PD. If Mike had been sober, he'd have noticed them the moment he stepped into the parking lot.

"You think you're such a goddamn hero, don't you?" Stevens swaggered forward. He balled his hands into fists. The tendons in his wiry arms stood out with iron-pumping definition. "You didn't even wait for us to go to trial before trying to sell your rat-bastard lies to Mr. Movie Star."

The pounding in Mike's ears grew louder, making his molars ache.

"Mr. Dead Movie Star," added the Moe of the group, Rodriguez. "Too bad for you."

Mike inhaled cool, dry air. He hadn't approached Nick Warner. It had been Warner who'd come up with the idea of putting Mike's story on the silver screen. Mike had told Warner's people to forget it every single one of the half-dozen times they'd called. Unfortunately, Hollywood megastars weren't used to hearing the word *no*. And when the film festival rolled around, Warner had shown up in Denver, as if challenging Mike to say no to that famous face in person.

Nick Warner had been shot to death before Mike had gotten the chance.

Mike turned away from the cops the *Denver Post* had dubbed "the Dirty Three" and kept his feet moving toward his motel room. He didn't want to have this conversation. Hollywood and the *Post* might think he was a hero for cleaning up corruption in the Denver PD, but he sure as hell didn't. He was more inclined to agree with his old man's assessment.

Traitor.

Not that he'd had much of a choice. Not if he wanted to uphold the law. Not if he wanted to do the right thing.

Either way, he had spent the night striving to forget everything that had happened in the past few months…hell, everything that had happened in the past twenty years. And the last thing he wanted was to ruin a good drunk by strolling down memory lane with the dirty three.

"Trying to run away? Can't face us without Internal Affairs by your side?" Rodriguez taunted. He nodded to the others.

On cue, Fisher stepped into his path, his linebacker shoulders blocking sight of the motel. Stevens and Rodriguez positioned themselves on either side.

Run away? If only he could. "Going to bed. Been a long day."

"Not as long as it's going to get," Fisher said.

Mike tipped his head back to meet Fisher's eyes. The parking lot seemed to sway under his feet.

"How much did you get for selling your story?" Rodriguez again.

"Who says I sold it?"

"The kind of money Hollywood throws around? You sold it."

Mike shook his head. Mistake. The whole world swirled around him. Of course they didn't believe he'd turned down the money. That's what had gotten them in trouble in the first place. Money. Greed. That's why they couldn't resist ripping off drug dealers. Easy cash, no victims. Not victims who didn't deserve what they got, at any rate. If it wasn't for greed, Fisher, Stevens and Rodriguez would still be on the job instead of on suspension awaiting the outcome of an investigation.

"We want a piece of that Hollywood cash."

"Can't help you."

Fisher balled a bus-sized hand into a fist. "You will."

"Or what? You going to assault me? You going to beat me to a pulp?" He was in a bad enough position already without taunting them, but he couldn't help it.

White teeth glowed against Fisher's dark face. "I don't see any witnesses."

True enough,

It was too late for traffic, yet still two hours shy of bar time. Mike was screwed. Not that he didn't deserve a beating. Hell, he'd deserved it since that afternoon when he was seventeen years old.

He focused on Fisher. He might as well get it over with, and the man mountain seemed most likely to end things quickly. Swaying slightly, he fisted a hand and smashed it straight into Fisher's nose.

The big man stepped backward, a bellow breaking from his lips.

Mike stumbled forward, carried by his own momentum, and ran smack into Fisher's return punch. He struggled to keep his balance, just as Rodriguez landed a punch to his kidney and Fisher thrust an elbow into his eye.

He hit the ground.

A boot connected with his mouth. Another slammed above his eye. Blow after blow bruised his ribs, his gut, his legs. He gasped for breath, taking in nothing but dust. Blood flooded his mouth, turning dust to mud, sticky and hot.

Ironic that his beating came at the hands

of brothers he had betrayed. Brothers he'd let down.

Fitting.

Another kick landed square, reverberating through his head, making his brain flicker to black.

Chapter Two

The whistling twitter of a bird cut through Mike's aching head, loud as a police siren. He considered lifting his head, then thought better of the idea. Every muscle in his body hurt. Gravel gouged his cheek and his mouth tasted like something had crawled in and died.

Maybe something had.

Gritting his teeth against the pounding in his skull, he forced his lids to open. Well, one lid. The other wouldn't budge, his eye swollen and aching to high hell.

The soft light of dawn glowed over the parking lot. Memories from the night before filtered through his sluggish mind. The argument with his dad. Shot after shot of mescal. The pummeling at the hands and boots of the Dirty Three.

A lovely evening all around.

Summoning what courage he had, he lifted his head from the gravel. Agony shot down the back of his neck. His stomach swirled in protest. But finally, breathing as if he'd just run ten miles, he worked his way to his feet and wobbled across the remaining ten feet to his motel-room door. Leaning against the jamb, he groped his pockets.

No key.

He'd had it after he left the bar. He was sure of it. He remembered holding the plastic key fob in his hand. Before he ran into his not-so-good buddies on the force, before they beat the crap out of him.

He swayed, brushing the door. It swung inward. Open.

Mike tensed. Darkness veiled the room's interior, but he could still make out the dark shape of his duffel, lying on the bed where he'd left it. A pair of jeans trailed from the open bag and draped onto the floor. If some bum had found the key in the lot and let himself in, he might still be inside. What Mike wouldn't give to have his weapon right now. Too bad he'd left it in the duffel. The duffel that someone had obviously ransacked.

He flattened himself against the door jamb and pushed the door wide.

He waited for a beat. Two beats. Three. No sound came from the room. No movement.

Here goes nothing. He moved into the doorway and peered inside.

The place seemed vacant enough. But the evidence that someone had gone through his things couldn't be more clear. The change of clothes and toothbrush Mike had shoved in the duffel were strewn across the bed. His razor glinted from where it lay on the worn carpet. And he didn't have to search through the shell of the duffel to see the worst of it— his service pistol was gone.

"UNTIL FURTHER NOTICE, you're on administrative leave pending investigation. I'm sorry, Lawson."

Mike squinted at Tim Grady's face through his swollen eye. Suspended for losing his gun. Stuck in a damn hospital room overnight for observation. *Sorry* was the right word. As in Mike Lawson was one sorry-assed son-of-a-bitch. "I suppose a lot of guys are finding this pretty funny."

"Well…" Tim Grady grinned, exposing the wide gap between his front teeth.

Mike suppressed a chuckle, afraid it would hurt his face, his head, his neck. Even though he'd worked with Grady for nearly three years, that gap in his partner's smile still cracked him up at the oddest times. It was endearing. Disarming. And it had come in handy more than once when they'd had to play good cop, bad cop with a suspect. Once Grady flashed that grin, he was everybody's friend. "Did the lieutenant think to ask the Dirty Three if they happened to come across my gun? Say, after they got tired of beating on me and let themselves into my motel room?"

"I don't know about the LT, but I did a little nosing around. Off the record."

Mike tried to raise an eyebrow in silent question, but the gesture turned into more of a flinch and groan. "And?"

"They say they didn't touch your key. That some lowlife must have come across you at bar time, taken the key and let himself into your motel room."

"And you believe them?"

"Like hell." Grady canted his head to one side. "Still, I don't see that taking your Sig buys them much."

"Makes me look bad."

"You did a pretty good job of that without their help. Why *were* you trying to drown yourself last night anyway? And what made you stupid enough to throw the first punch?"

Mike rested his head back on his pillow. "Damn. What the hell am I doing stuck here? All I need is a few stitches and a pack of ice."

Grady shook his head. "You don't want to talk about it? Fine with me. Take the time the lieutenant gave you. Get your head straight. God knows the time I took after Janey died sure helped me. Besides, I don't want some messed-up cop with a death wish watching my back, thank you very much." Grady smiled, but even that gap couldn't mitigate the hard ring of his words.

Mike closed his aching eyes. Grady had been through hell with his wife's illness and subsequent death and yet he'd pulled himself together. So why couldn't Mike seem to manage it?

Suspended from the job, Mike had nothing but time. Too bad all the time in the world wouldn't change anything. He'd had twenty years to try to chip away at the guilt that calcified inside him, and if anything it had grown harder, despite his best efforts to always do the right thing. Time might have helped Grady, but for Mike a few weeks of vacation wasn't going to make a dent.

"Excuse me. Detective Lawson?" A mellow female voice cut through Mike's thoughts.

He opened his eyes.

An elegant blonde stood in the doorway, her long wavy hair falling over the shoulders of her light gray business suit. She skewered him with a cool blue gaze.

"Mrs. Prescott." Mike hadn't seen Evangeline Prescott since he'd last worked as liaison between the Denver PD and her company, Prescott Personal Securities, on a protected-witness case over six months ago. She was a classy woman who ran a classy organization. And although she had suffered the loss of her husband, Robert, in a plane crash two years before, she, too, had managed to pull her life together after tragedy.

"Please, call me Evangeline." She stepped into the room. Behind her, and five inches shorter, a woman with curly auburn hair that just brushed her shoulders followed. A concerned look flashed across her pretty features as she took in his battered face.

Mike's adrenaline spiked.

"You remember Cassie Allen, Detective?" Evangeline said.

As if he would forget Cassie. As if he could. He forced his aching face into some semblance of a smile. Raising his hands, he formed his stiff fingers into the shapes that were still second nature to him, even after all these years. *Hi, Cassie.*

She returned his smile for a split second, then pressed her lips tight and studied the pattern of tile on the floor.

She didn't look happy to be there, that was for sure. A fact that bothered him more than it should. It wasn't as if they'd had anything beyond a working relationship on the occasions he'd dealt with Prescott Personal Securities. But still… "Evangeline and Cassie, this is Detective Tim Grady."

"I'm sorry if we're interrupting." Evangeline glanced at Grady.

Grady thrust himself free of the wall. "Nah, I gotta get going. Bad guys wait for no one

and all that. Nice meeting the two of you."
With a gap-toothed grin, Grady was gone.

Evangeline focused on Mike. "I don't want
to waste your time or ours, Detective, so I'll
tell you why we're here. I want you to work
for me."

Surely the pounding in his head had inter-
fered with his hearing. "Work for you?"

"The grapevine has it that you're on leave
from the police department."

"Bad news sure travels fast."

"And whenever a door closes, a window
opens," she said, matching his cliché. "I need
someone who is honest. Someone I can
trust."

"For what?"

"A very sensitive case. There's a briefing at
our offices tomorrow morning. I'll give you
the details then. If you can't make it, Cassie
will fill you in. You'll be working with her."
Evangeline watched his expression as though
she knew full well how much the prospect of
working with Cassie would appeal to him.

He looked past those knowing blue eyes
and focused on Cassie's warm brown ones.

Cassie shook her head with a snap of

frustration. No doubt she'd read Evangeline's lips and had her own thoughts about the assignment. Her hands flew, signing her thoughts behind her boss's back. *She wants you to be my bodyguard. The poor little deaf girl's babysitter. A babysitter I don't need. Feel free to turn her down. It's not a good use of your time.*

Mike frowned at Evangeline. It didn't add up. None of it. Even if Cassie was right, and Evangeline merely wanted someone to look after her cute little computer whiz, that didn't explain why she would pick him. "You shouldn't believe all my recent press. I'm no hero."

"Don't worry. I don't believe everything I read."

"Then why me?" He gestured to his face. "I'm a drunk."

"One night of drinking doesn't a drunk make. I know more about you than you think, Detective Lawson."

"Then you know that half the police department hates me. You know I'm suspended for losing my gun. Surely you can come up with a better bodyguard prospect at PPS."

"I'm sure I can. But not for this case. I trust

you. You're honest and I know you'll remain honest…even when it's inconvenient."

Inconvenient? If only that was all betraying fellow cops was, an inconvenience.

"But that's only part of it."

He waited for her to go on.

"You've worked with Cassie before. You're able to communicate."

You can talk to the poor little deaf girl. Cassie's fingers stabbed the air. *Really, I don't need you. I can handle this myself.*

"I know some sign language and I can imagine the rest." Evangeline glanced at Cassie. One side of her lips tilted up in a knowing smile. She turned her focus back to Mike. "What Cassie doesn't realize is that I would provide a bodyguard for any technician I had working on this particular case. Hearing or not. It just works well that the two of you can communicate. And that you worked well together in the past."

Working with Cassie wasn't his concern. That part sounded great. Too good to be true. And *that's* what worried him. "I come with a lot of baggage."

"We can work around that."

"I don't think you quite get the picture. The

Denver Post might think I'm a hero, but half the police department would like to see me fall on my face."

Evangeline waved away his protest with a manicured hand. "I know you're no longer in a position to be my go-between with the Denver PD. That's not what I'm hiring you to do."

"You don't get it. Some are so eager to see me fall, they're waiting in line to give me a shove."

"Then you'll have to keep your balance. I'll add that to your job duties."

It was impossible to argue with this woman. But then she and her late husband, Robert Prescott, hadn't gotten where they were by taking no for an answer. It seemed there was a lot of that going around. "What are my duties? If I were to accept, that is."

"Cassie will be working on deciphering an encrypted disk. It's very important. Very sensitive. I want you to provide security while she does the work."

See? Babysitter, Cassie signed. *Tell her to forget it.*

He tried to keep his expression neutral. He had a bad feeling about this. He hadn't exaggerated when he'd said a good portion of the

Denver PD would like to make him pay for blowing the whistle on the Dirty Three's racket of stealing profits from drug dealers. Not to mention the Dirty Three themselves. He doubted they would be satisfied with one friendly little beating. They'd find any way they could to make his life as miserable as he'd made theirs. And he sure as hell didn't want Cassie to get caught in the crossfire. "I still don't understand why you don't deal with this in-house. Why hire freelance bodyguards?"

"Not *bodyguards*. Just you. Just this case."

Cassie shook her head. *There's going to be nothing for you to do but sit and stare at me while I work.*

He stifled a smile. The only way that argument would succeed was if she was trying to talk him *into* taking the job.

Tell her no, Cassie signed.

"I can arrange for someone to fill in if you need a day or two to clear your schedule," Evangeline said.

His schedule? What a laugh. Though he supposed he could fill a lot of hours drinking and feeling sorry for himself. "It's not that."

"I'm prepared to beat your salary at the Denver PD."

"It's not money, either."

Evangeline stepped forward so Cassie was fully behind her. "We need you, Detective. Cassie needs you. If I can't rely on you to protect her, I'm going to have to find someone else to decode that disk."

"If the damn thing is so dangerous, that might not be a bad idea."

"Okay. You tell her."

"Excuse me?"

"You can tell Cassie she's off the case. You can tell her her inability to hear makes it too dangerous for her to do this job without someone to watch her back. You tell her."

A lump the size of a fist tightened in his gut. During the past cases he'd worked with Cassie, he'd come to understand how important her work was to her. How vital it was that she was treated like everyone else. How much she deplored being singled out or coddled for her disability. And how much the news that she was being taken off this obviously important case would kill her.

But being killed figuratively was better than being killed for real.

He eyed Cassie and formed the words with

his hands. *If this case is so dangerous, maybe you shouldn't take it on.*

She shook her head. *I'm decrypting the disk. I'm the best at PPS when it comes to decryption. I'll be careful. I'm not stupid.*

No, she was definitely not stupid. He gave her a smile.

"Take the job, Detective," Evangeline prodded. "We'll work around the problems with those few officers at the Denver PD. Cassie needs you."

He shook his head. "She doesn't need me."

"Okay, maybe she doesn't need you. But you can't argue with the fact that right now, you need this case."

The macho cop inside him wanted to say he didn't need this case or any other. That he didn't need anything…or anybody. But Mike knew that was a lie. He'd been struggling since he'd informed Internal Affairs about the Dirty Three. Struggling with guilt, with his damn conscience, with the fantasy of drinking his problems away. Last night proved that. The only thing that had kept him together was the job. And now that he didn't have that, he didn't have anything.

He looked past Evangeline and focused on Cassie. He'd been attracted to her curly auburn hair and sassy little body since he'd first laid eyes on her. But it was more than that. The whole act of talking to her, using his hands to form letters, watching her convey her thoughts with gestures and expressions...being around her took him back in time. Before the horrible mistake he'd made that summer day when he was seventeen. Before the guilt and self-loathing. She made him feel that he had a chance to rewrite the past.

And how could he pass up an opportunity like that?

Chapter Three

"Who's that?"

Cassie watched Angel's black-lipsticked lips form the words between chews on her ever-present wad of gum. It was amazing the gum didn't get caught on the silver ball piercing her tongue.

Cassie shrugged and brought her attention back to the copy machine Angel had managed to break for the third time this month. She had an important case to attend to, protocols to decipher, algorithms to test. She didn't have time for fixing machines and speculating about the face on the reception area's security monitor. Knowing Angel, she could be talking about the UPS man and had just forgotten what he looked like since the delivery he'd made the day before.

"I'd sure like to meet him. He's hot."

Not the UPS man. He was cute, but at five-foot-nothing and prematurely balding, Cassie doubted Angel would call him hot. Of course, if he traded in his brown shorts for black and threw in multiple piercings, who knew?

Angel grabbed Cassie's arm, long black talons poking through her cotton sweater. "You got to look, Cass. Tell me what you think."

Cassie sighed. There was no use ignoring Angel at times. The PPS receptionist was a force. A force that broke copy machines and had apparently decided Cassie was her buddy. Probably because Cassie didn't talk back.

Abandoning the copier, Cassie stuck her head around the cubicle wall separating the copy/fax area from the rest of reception.

Mike Lawson peered from the security monitor. Purple bruises covered his jaw and crept up one cheek. One eye was ringed in black and purple like a cartoon cliché. And other than the purple and black and angry red scrapes, he was pale as the snowcaps on the mountains. He looked like the undead. No wonder Angel found him hot.

Not that Cassie did or anything.

She tried to ignore the warm tremor that danced in her stomach seemingly every time she saw the tall, dark and serious cop. There was only one explanation for his presence at PPS this morning. He must have decided to take Evangeline up on her job offer.

Great.

Evangeline wouldn't be this concerned about a hearing technician deciphering a disk. William Leonard, or Lenny as everyone called him, the senior technician at PPS had worked on countless intricate cases and never once had Evangeline insisted he have a baby-sitter.

A flush of anger heated her cheeks. Would she never be allowed to show what she was capable of doing? Would well-meaning people always insist on coddling the deaf girl?

She glanced at Angel. She didn't know what the receptionist was waiting for, but she hadn't taken a step out of the copy area. She set the toner cartridge she was holding on a nearby countertop and turned to Angel, making her signs so simple and clear that even Angel could understand. *Why don't you greet him?*

Angel shook her head hard, her black,

spiked do so stiff with spray not a single hair moved. "Me?"

Angel picked the damnedest times to start being shy. *It's your job. You're the receptionist.*

"Oh, yeah, you're right." Angel ducked out of the printing and fax area and scampered to her desk.

As soon as Angel left, Cassie made her way down a short hall to the glassed-in area that protected the servers and most of the tech equipment at PPS from the dust and hustle of the offices and cubicles where the agents worked. She slipped behind a bank of servers.

She wasn't ready to face Mike Lawson. Just one glimpse of him in the reception desk monitor made her feel as jittery as a teenage girl. Not the feeling she was after. This was the first case she'd worked on solo, the first time Evangeline had trusted her with something really big. She needed to prove she could do as good a job as any hearing person. A better job. And being around Mike Lawson, having him babysit her, didn't make her feel exactly capable.

A gentle hand tapped her shoulder.

She whirled around to face Lenny, her

brilliant coworker who all but ran the technology department. His fire-red hair stuck out in several spots, as if he'd slept at his desk last night instead of going home. Again. No one was as dedicated as Lenny.

"Who are you hiding from?" Lenny's lips formed the words.

My bodyguard, she signed.

He gave her an odd look. Lenny might be brilliant, but he wasn't as well versed in relating to humans as he was relating to computers. He probably thought she really was hiding from her bodyguard.

Well, wasn't she?

She stepped out from behind the servers. *Just kidding,* she signed.

Lenny nodded as if he still didn't understand. "It's cool you have a bodyguard. I mean you work to protect other people's bodies, it's about time someone protects yours, right? You're lucky." He shrugged a skinny shoulder.

Lucky? Her fingers raced. *I don't want to be lucky. I want to be respected.*

The grin fell from Lenny's freckled face and he stared at her blankly.

She took a deep breath. Whenever she got upset, she signed too fast for anyone at PPS to keep up. Even poor Lenny the genius couldn't keep track of her flying fingers. But she hated speaking out loud. Just the thought that other people could hear her voice and she couldn't made her feel uncomfortably out of control.

She let out a sigh. *Never mind. I'm just blowing off steam.*

Lenny offered her an awkward smile, as if he still didn't understand her but didn't want to be rude enough to say so, and shuffled back to his workstation.

Cassie watched him go, guilt clamping down on her shoulders. Of course Lenny would think having a bodyguard was cool. He was working on sensitive projects, too, yet he had no bodyguard. Further evidence Evangeline was going out of her way to take care of the deaf girl.

The change in air flow alerted her to the open door. She glanced over to find herself face-to-face with Mike Lawson.

Angel was right. Even with the battered face and swollen eye, he was hot. A fact that only made this moment all the more awkward.

Don't look so excited, he signed.

She gave him a frown.

Which way to the large conference room?

The briefing. Of course. She'd been so shaken about Mike Lawson's appearance, she'd all but forgotten the case. Her first big case. Her chance to prove what she could do.

She marched to the conference room, feeling Mike's presence behind her even though she couldn't hear his footfalls on the terra-cotta tile. She pushed through the conference room's double doors. The large conference table stretched in front of them, empty chairs ringing its circumference.

Where were the other agents? Had she gotten the wrong conference room?

Evangeline breezed through the door behind them. "Shall we get started?"

Cassie frowned in her boss's direction. *Where is everyone?*

"The disk's decryption concerns only the two of you. Please take a seat. We need to get started." Evangeline focused on Mike. "Glad you decided to take me up on my offer, Detective. After yesterday, I wasn't sure you'd make it."

"Funny. I got the feeling you were far too sure."

Cassie tore her gaze from Mike's lips and

slipped into the closest chair. Mike folded himself into the seat next to her. Evangeline strode to the head of the table and punched a few buttons on the laptop. An image materialized on the screen in front of them. Movie star Nick Warner gazed from the screen with fierce determination in a famous scene from his action film *Sayonara, Baby*.

Cassie felt Mike shift beside her.

Evangeline gave Mike a pointed look. "I'm sure the two of you have heard about Nick Warner's death."

Mike glowered.

Cassie didn't know what was going on, but it was clear Mike wasn't expecting Evangeline's reference to the deceased movie star. And he wasn't happy about it.

His lips tightened as they formed the words. "Is that why you wanted me on this case? Something to do with Warner?"

Evangeline returned his gaze unfazed. "I wanted you on the case for the reasons I gave you. Of course, any knowledge you have about Nick Warner will be appreciated."

"I don't know anything about him."

"I heard he came to the Denver film festival at least partially to meet with you."

"I never spoke to him."

"You did talk to people who worked for him, though." Evangeline's expression made it clear she was not asking a question but stating a fact.

It seemed there was more to Evangeline's selection of Mike as her bodyguard than his knowledge of American Sign Language. Much more. Cassie watched Mike for an answer.

"I talked to them long enough to tell them I was not going to let them option my story, no matter what they paid me."

"Who did you talk to? Specifically?"

Mike shifted in his chair, as if the answer made him uncomfortable. "Mitchell Caruthers."

Evangeline nodded. "You know, Caruthers set Nick Warner up to be killed?"

"It doesn't surprise me."

"He endangered Nick, his wife and their four-year-old daughter."

Cassie had heard the talk about Nick's wife and little girl. Even neck deep in computers, she couldn't miss that story. Especially the gossip about the budding relationship between the widowed Mrs. Warner and PPS agent Jack Sanders.

"Specifically, Detective, do you remember Caruthers mentioning anything to you about a list?"

"A list? A list of what?"

"That's what we need to know."

"Listen, I don't know anything about Caruthers beyond the fact that he said he worked for Nick Warner. He said nothing to me about a list."

Cassie eyed Evangeline. *How did you hear about this list?* she signed.

"Caruthers told Jack." Evangeline glanced at Mike. "Agent Jack Sanders, that is. He referred to it as a list of names. Jack thinks it has something to do with investments Caruthers made with money he stole from Nick Warner. Unfortunately that's about all we know. We have no idea if this list contains the names of investors, or the names of companies or what exactly. But I aim to find out."

Is that what is on the disk? Cassie signed the question.

"Perhaps. Perhaps it's something else entirely. The disk showed up at our office after Nick Warner's death. But we don't know who sent it. Or what data it contains. I guess you'll have to decipher it to find out how it's connected to this list. Or if it's connected at all."

"But you think it is connected," Mike said.

Evangeline nodded. "The timing was too much of a coincidence. And I don't believe in coincidences."

Neither did Cassie.

"There's more." Evangeline focused on Mike. "Caruthers mentioned a specific name in connection to all of this. Milo Kardascian."

Mike frowned. "The CEO of Vasco Pharmaceuticals."

"The same." She tapped a key on her computer and the screens in front of them flashed a picture of the multimillionaire.

Cassie recognized the man's prominent flat nose and heavy jowls. PPS had provided security at parties he'd attended. She'd worked on the technical support end of the surveillance teams, though she didn't know much about Kardascian personally. Just that the hard look in his eyes had given her the creeps. *How is he involved in this?* she asked.

Evangeline focused her attention on Cassie. "That's what we need to find out. He might know something about this list, or something about the cipher or ciphers needed to read that disk. I've had no luck reaching Mr. Kardascian, but I have it from a reliable source that he's vacationing in his cabin west of Denver. I need you to visit him in person, find out what he knows."

Cassie straightened in her seat. *I can go while the computer is running my next set of algorithms.*

"The two of you can go."

The two of them? Wasn't that overkill? What was Mike supposed to do? Hold her hand? *I don't need a bodyguard to talk to the CEO of a respected company.*

Evangeline shook her head. "Actually, you might be happy to have that bodyguard around Mr. Kardascian. Isn't that right, Detective Lawson?"

Cassie turned to look at Mike.

A muscle tensed along his jaw. "Don't tell me. You also brought me aboard because I'm acquainted with Milo Kardascian, or is that just a coincidence, too?"

Evangeline gave a calm smile in answer. "Any additional questions or comments?"

Cassie had dozens of comments. Though

she doubted any of them would change Evangeline's mind.

"Good. Report back to me after you talk to Kardascian. Don't let her out of your sight, Detective. And, Cassie?"

The terse look on Evangeline's face caused a hitch in Cassie's stomach. She raised her eyebrows at her boss, conveying the fact that she understood. And was listening.

"Do your job. Nothing more. I need you back here in one piece to run those decryption programs."

CASSIE WHIRLED to face Mike as soon as they pulled out of the PPS underground parking garage. *What do you know about Milo Kardascian? What isn't Evangeline telling me?*

Kardascian. Not one of Mike's favorite topics.

Hands on the steering wheel, he turned his head toward Cassie, to give her a clear view of his lips. "He's not a nice guy."

She stared, waiting for him to go on.

"He has a nasty habit of beating up women. When I was still on patrol, I was called to his house at the Polo Grounds a few times." He didn't need to tell her the rest. Ancient history. And not one of his prouder moments.

He caught the movement of Cassie's fingers from the corner of his eye.

Then he'll be defensive around you. I'll ask him the questions.

He'd known from the first time he'd met Cassie that she was independent. He hadn't realized she had a chip on her shoulder the size of the Rocky Mountain range. "Listen, I'm betting a self-absorbed bastard like Kardascian doesn't know one word in ASL. How are you going to ask him anything?"

"I can talk when I have to."

Her voice sounded low and rich. The inflections were a little flat, but her voice was still the sexiest he'd ever heard. He'd forgotten Cassie hadn't always been deaf, unlike Tommy, who'd been deaf from birth. "Why don't you talk more? You have a great voice."

I don't like not knowing how I sound, she said, back to using her hands.

"You sound beautiful. Sexy." He didn't know what had made him admit that out loud. He and Cassie were working together, not dating. He needed to keep things all business between them. And besides, even if something could happen between them, he didn't need to add letting Cassie down to his list of screwups. But even knowing all that, the words had slipped out and he hadn't wanted to bite them back.

She shook her head as if impatient with him. *Regardless of how my voice sounds, I can make him understand me just fine. Don't worry.*

At least one of them had her head together. At least where aimless flirting was concerned. "Kardascian not being able to understand you is only one problem with you questioning him."

I can handle him.

Maybe she could, maybe she couldn't. Nothing against Cassie, but he wasn't about to let her try. "It's my job to protect you, Cassie. You're going to have to let me do it."

Her fingers flew with lightning speed. *I've been working on the disk. I know more of the background on the case. I will be the one asking the questions. I'm good at my job, Detective. Just because I can't hear—*

"Whoa. Wait a minute. You might want to twist this into an argument about your deafness, but that has nothing to do with why I don't want you near Kardascian. He's one brutal bastard. Pure and simple. I can protect you. And damn it, I'm going to. You're in charge of decryption, and I'll take care of Kardascian and anything else that's dangerous. If you have a problem with that, take it up with Evangeline."

She crinkled her eyebrows and turned her head away, peering out the window at the foothills and gullies scrolling past. Auburn curls draped over her cheek, shielding her face from view.

So much for making his point. He wasn't sure she'd chosen to take in a word he said. With a hearing woman, he could make her listen, or at least drone on for his own amusement. Cassie could shut him out with the turn of her head. There was nothing he could do to bring her focus back to him…unless he grasped her arm and physically turned her.

He pushed that idea as far from his mind as he could get it. He was attracted enough to Cassie Allen. He sure didn't need to add physical contact into the equation.

The pavement curved south and climbed sharply. He focused on the road ahead, squinting into the sun. Pain stabbed his swollen eye like an ice pick jamming into his brain. At least he no longer had a hangover. Yesterday the sun would have killed him.

At least *that* would have made Cassie happy.

Twenty silent minutes later, they crested the ridge. He located the address and wound down the long driveway. Kardascian's mansion hung on the side of the mountain, a log cabin with so much glass it was hard to figure out just where logs came into play. "Pharmaceuticals pay well, that's for damn sure," he said to himself.

He parked near the front walk and climbed from the car. By the time he'd circled to the passenger side, Cassie was out and smoothing her skirt with the palms of her hands. He stepped in front of her so she would have to look at him. "Are we on the same page?"

She pressed her lips together. Setting her chin, she stepped around him and marched up the stairs.

So much for their argument on the drive. He started after her, drawing even before she reached the front door. Extending a finger, he stabbed the doorbell.

The chime echoed through the house. The

sound died, leaving only the spring chatter of birds and wind whistling through aspens and evergreen bows.

Cassie punched the doorbell, the chimes ringing a second time.

Still no answer. Mike stepped through the carefully landscaped bed surrounding the front step and cupped his hand against the garage window to shield the sun's reflection. The red gleam of a convertible Corvette shone from one of the bays. A heavy-duty SUV hulked in another. And in the third, a chrome-decked Harley. Only a fraction of his vehicle collection. The rest must be at his high-rise condo in Denver, the place he'd moved after signing his house at the Polo Grounds over to his ex-wife. Or maybe one of his other half-dozen homes.

Whatever his vehicle situation, the lack of empty garage bays didn't mean he wasn't driving a different expensive vehicle. Or that he didn't use a car service. But there was something else about the garage that bothered Mike. Something that didn't feel right.

The door. He looked closer. Sure enough, the door from garage to house was open. A minute ticked by, yet no movement came from the house. He focused on that open door. A smudge of something marred the pristine white steel just below the knob. Something brownish…

Blood?

There were a myriad of other possible explanations—dirt, chocolate, who knew what? But that didn't explain the bad feeling chomping at the back of Mike's neck like an attack dog. He signed to Cassie. *Go back to the car. I'm going to take a look around.*

Cassie shook her head.

Damn. He might be paranoid, but he couldn't take the chance. The last thing he needed was for Cassie to get caught up in something bad. He wasn't going to let that happen. *This could be serious, Cassie. And you're unarmed. I might have had my badge suspended, but at least I have my personal weapon. You're going to have to do what I say. Go back to the car, lock yourself in and call 9-1-1. If anything happens, get the hell out of here.* He tossed her the keys.

She caught them, hesitated, then nodded.

Mike waited until he saw her climb into the

car, slam the door and hit the electronic locks before he circled the house.

The house's doors were locked, windows secured. If he had a real reason to believe someone was in imminent danger inside, he'd break a window and let himself in. As it was, a hunch didn't cut it with the law. He was already going out on a limb by calling the sheriff's department out here all based on a brownish smudge and a bad feeling.

He circled the side of the log cabin. Four windows cut into the logs on this side of the house. He peered inside each one. A formal living room. A study. Rich earth-toned furniture, plush carpet and rough-hewn stone fireplaces decorated each space. The rooms looked spotless and utterly vacant, as if the only one who ever set foot in the place was the cleaning lady.

So why had she missed the smudge on the inside garage door?

After he'd circled about half the house, the ground fell away into a steep slope. Decking loomed overhead, arranged in three layers. The entire back of the house was glass, gleaming in the sunlight.

Mike stepped to the sliding glass door

on the lowest level and peered inside. A shape loomed dark against white carpet. A prone body.

Gripping either side of the door, Mike fought the sliding door free of its lock and lifted it off the track. An alarm screamed through the house. He scanned the room for movement as he raced to the body.

Kardascian.

Blood bloomed from the millionaire's chest, soaking his thick cotton sweatshirt and seeping into the white berber. His labored breathing rasped raw in the silence.

The bullet must have pierced a lung. The man was drowning in his own blood.

Grabbing the sweatshirt, Mike shoved it up Kardascian's thick torso, exposing a small gunshot wound oozing blood. He needed something airtight to seal the hole in the lung. And he needed it now.

He sprang to his feet and scanned the room. Weight machines of every type imaginable dotted the space. A covered hot tub filled the adjacent room, visible through glass doors. A wet bar nestled in the corner.

Mike raced for the wet bar. He rifled through cupboards until he found a box of garbage bags. Pulling one free, he headed back to Kardascian.

Please, let him still be alive.

The CEO's breath rasped, bubbling through blood.

Mike fitted the plastic bag tight to the wound. Centering his weight over the man, he pressed down on Kardascian's chest. "Hold on, man. You're going to pull through this."

The sucking sound stopped. So far, so good. But Mike had no way of knowing how much blood was already in Kardascian's lungs. Judging from the gurgling sound, it wasn't a small amount.

The millionaire watched him through glassy eyes. He opened his mouth, straining for breath. Fighting. He thrashed his hands weakly, already slipping away.

Mike adjusted his weight, trying to keep up the pressure. The carpet squished beneath him. How much blood had Kardascian lost?

A gasp cut through the room.

Mike looked up and into Cassie's rounded eyes. "Did you call for help?"

She nodded. She raced to his side, obviously eager to do something, anything to assist him. But there wasn't anything she could do. There wasn't anything either of them could do. Milo Kardascian was dead.

Chapter Four

Mike stood in front of Milo Kardascian's garage and watched the Denver Police Department SUV wind around curves and down the slope on its way to the cabin. He'd already answered a slew of questions from the Jefferson County sheriff's deputy who'd arrived on the scene first. He'd thought the worst thing that could happen at this point was to be asked to relive his failure to save Kardascian's life one more time. He was wrong. Explaining why he was in this situation to the lieutenant promised to be even more miserable.

Denver PD? Cassie's fingers trembled slightly as she signed, but other than that, she seemed more pulled together than he felt. *Why is the Denver PD here? Isn't this outside their jurisdiction?*

It's my lieutenant.

Cassie searched his face. *Is that bad?*

I wish I knew. And that was the part that was driving him nuts. He was used to being on the inside during a scene like this. Gathering evidence. Talking to the medical examiner. Having officers and experts report to him. Standing around waiting for the next bout of questions with no clue what was going on was killing him.

Especially when they seemed to be treating him as more suspect than witness.

He shifted his feet on the concrete apron in front of the garage. No point in venting all that to Cassie. She'd been through too much already this morning. She sure didn't need more to worry about on top of it. *How are you holding up?*

She gave him an unconvincing smile. *Fine. Right.*

Okay, not so fine. I've never seen someone die before. Especially someone who was murdered. And all the blood. Her shoulders hitched with a small shudder. *I'm still feeling a little shaken, I guess.*

Hell, who could blame her? Even though he'd seen more than his share of dead bodies, he was shuddering right along with her. Not enough to notice, but he could feel the tremor deep in his bones.

Maybe a man dying under your fingertips did that to you.

He resisted the urge to look down at his stained hands, Kardascian's blood dark in the creases of his skin, or his jeans, the denim now as stiff as if it had been sprayed with starch. *I'm sorry you had to go through all this.*

I'm just glad you were there with me so I didn't have to face it alone. One side of her lips quirked upward in some semblance of a half smile. *No matter what I said before.*

You're welcome. I wish I could do more. Like get you out of here. He raked a hand through his hair. *If I only knew what the hell was going on.*

Maybe the lieutenant will let you know what they've found. Cassie focused clear eyes on the SUV, as if she believed that by positive thinking and the force of will she could influence the mind of the man inside. *Maybe he'll convince the county to let us go home.*

Mike wasn't going to hold his breath for that to happen. But he wasn't about to dash Cassie's hopes, either. *Maybe so.*

The SUV came to a stop behind the boxy, tan sheriff's cars and three doors swung open. The LT, Tim Grady and a veteran officer named Hawley climbed out and threaded their way to the sidewalk. Grady gave Mike a gap-toothed grin, the worried lines in his forehead canceling the comic value of his smile. The lieutenant and Officer Hawley passed without a glance.

The contingent of Denver PD climbed the steps to the front entrance of the elaborate cabin and joined the huddle of sheriff's men. The LT nodded his graying head as they filled him in.

Mike felt like crawling out of his skin. What he wouldn't give to be part of that huddle. What he wouldn't give to know what they were saying right now.

He eyed Cassie, then glanced back to the group of cops.

Cassie touched his arm. *What?* she signed.

He checked himself. It wasn't a very nice idea. Definitely not an ethical one. And something he shouldn't even be thinking in connection to Cassie, let alone be presenting to her. *Nothing.*

You're wondering if I can read their lips?

Hell, she could read more than lips. She could read his mind. *Not a good idea.*

She shrugged a shoulder. A mischievous smile curved the corners of her mouth and twinkled in her eyes. *Why not? If they were talking loud enough for you to overhear, wouldn't you listen?*

No, I wouldn't, he signed.

She gave a derisive snort. *Sure. And if you couldn't avoid it, you would keep whatever it is to yourself. You wouldn't think to tell me.*

He shook his head, trying to keep his serious expression in place. As much as he wanted to know what was going on, as much as he enjoyed seeing the mischievous glint replace the shell-shocked look in Cassie's eyes, he really couldn't let her get any more involved than she already was. *Really, Cassie, you're tangled up enough in this mess. Besides, it's not ethical.*

She tilted her head to the side and studied him. *You really are as honest as Evangeline says, aren't you?*

He looked down at the concrete apron under his feet. How in the hell was he supposed to answer that one? *I'm a cop.*

"Well, I'm not," she said out loud.

When he returned his gaze to her face, he wasn't surprised to see she was watching the deputies brief his lieutenant. A tall county sheriff's detective with a craggy face and salt-and-pepper hair spoke slowly and deliberately. His lips had to be a piece of cake for Cassie to read, even from this distance.

So much for his worry over her getting more involved.

They determined the path of entry was through the sliding glass door in the workout room. Cassie translated what she was seeing into sign language. *Never mind that we told them we came in that way,* she added.

Mike couldn't prevent a chuckle from escaping. Cassie was handling this whole ordeal with humor and attitude that surprised him. She certainly could roll with difficult circumstances. Probably better than he could.

They talked to Evangeline, Cassie continued. *She confirmed that we were here to talk to Mr. Kardascian about a case for PPS...but when they asked to see her client files, she told them to get a warrant.*

That Evangeline was a tough cookie. Mike would expect nothing less. The prospect of trying to get information out of her was almost enough to make him grateful he wasn't on the investigation end of this case...almost. As long as his hunch was wrong and he wasn't a suspect.

Officer Hawley turned away from the group. He surveyed the cabin, pausing on Mike. His eyes latched on to Cassie just as she commenced signing.

Damn.

They found something. Cassie's fingers flew.

Mike laid a hand on her arm.

She held up a hand and nodded that she saw him, but she didn't tear her gaze from the sheriff's detective's lips and she didn't still her hands. *Something in the bushes outside the glass door.*

Hawley started toward them.

They found a weapon...the murder weapon...a gun... She turned to look at Mike, her eyes wide.

Oh, hell.

"What is she doing?" Hawley closed in on them. "She's reading lips, isn't she? She's reporting every word."

On the sidewalk, the cluster of cops broke

up. The LT and Grady stayed on the sidewalk, two deputies headed their way.

Mike held up his hands, trying to head off the thuggish Denver PD officer. "Back off, Hawley."

Cassie just stared at Mike as if oblivious to Hawley or the sheriff's deputies, a stricken look on her face.

Hawley reached for Cassie's arm. "Ma'am, you're going to have to come with me."

Mike took a step forward. "She doesn't have to go anywhere."

"Who are you to decide a damn thing, Lawson? You're suspended. You're not even a cop anymore. If you were ever really a cop in the first place."

Good. At least Hawley's focus was on him, not Cassie. "What do you mean by that?"

An ugly sneer twisted Hawley's handsome face. "Cops don't sell out their own."

"Whoa. Hold on." The county detective caught up to Hawley, shooting him a look as if to remind him he was in the county's jurisdiction and he'd better know his place. "Your lieutenant wants to see you."

Officer Ted Hawley might be a jerk, but he had the good sense to retreat, even though all of them knew the LT hadn't said a word. Mike eyed the county man. "What's going down, Detective?"

"Lawson, you need to take a trip to the sheriff's offices with us."

Mike's gut plummeted. In his mind's eye, he replayed the look Cassie had given him. Shock. Fear. He hadn't been able to pay attention with Hawley homing in, but he thought it had something to do with the gun they'd found. The murder weapon. His gun? The service pistol he'd lost? Was that it? He eyed the detective. "Why? What's going on?"

"Come with me and I'll fill you in on the details."

More like he'd interrogate him eight ways from Sunday. Damn. Mike had been wanting more information, but being the suspect in this investigation was a bit more inside than he had in mind. Next time he really had to be more careful about what he wished for. "Should I call my union representative?"

"You really want to lawyer up, Lawson? Or would you rather clear this up?"

The same question he'd ask if a suspect started making noises about calling in legal representation. Mike glanced at Cassie. Still, if he went willingly and didn't piss the detective off, maybe he could keep Cassie out of this mess. "I'll go. But Ms. Allen doesn't have anything to do with this. Someone needs to take her back to the Prescott Personal Securities office."

The county detective's expression was a perfect blank. "Sorry. We need to talk to her, too."

CASSIE'S FINGERS SHOOK as she signed the same thing to the blank-faced sheriff's deputy for what had to be the fifth time. *Mike Lawson didn't kill that man.*

The deputy shook his head. "I'm sorry, ma'am. I don't understand what you're trying to tell me. If you'll just take a seat, I'll see if I can contact someone who knows sign language."

Cassie pushed out a frustrated breath. After a few cursory questions, the deputy who had transported her to the Jefferson County Sheriff's Department in Golden had told her she was free to go. In the two hours since, she'd been trying to get someone to listen to her pleas of Mike's innocence. Meanwhile they were raking Mike over the coals for the murder of a man he'd tried to save.

She forced her voice to work, feeling the uncertain vibration in her vocal chords. "Mike Lawson didn't kill that man."

He gave her a gentle smile. No, not gentle. Patronizing. Pitying. The reason she hated to speak out loud.

"You already spoke to a detective, didn't you?"

"Yes. But he didn't listen."

"I assure you, he listened. And he'll get in touch with you if he has any more questions or concerns. You gave him your contact information? Your home address?" He rounded his mouth with each word, speaking deliberately as if to a frightened child. One who couldn't speak English. And she'd just bet that his voice was raised to the level of a shout, as well.

Cassie felt like growling. She'd bet that would inspire an interesting response in this guy. "He has my home address, my work address and every other type of contact information known to man. What he doesn't have is the truth."

"That is what the investigation is for, ma'am."

"No kidding."

"Listen, I don't know what you expect me to do. Now if you'll excuse me, I have a job." Another pitying smile and the deputy walked away.

Cassie ground her teeth. She didn't know what she expected, either. But whatever it was, it didn't have anything to do with a good man being blamed for a murder he didn't commit.

The shock that had rocketed through her when she'd read the officer's lips at the scene was still sending aftershocks through her arms and legs. Mike's gun found at the scene…Mike's gun recently fired…Mike's gun…

It was ridiculous. Mike was an honest cop. Hell, he was the poster boy for honest cops. How could they think he'd killed Milo Kardascian?

A light touch on her shoulder jolted through her. She whirled around and looked into the face of one of the cops who'd been at Kardascian's cabin. The cop she'd first seen in Mike's hospital room. Mike's partner, Tim Grady.

"I'm sorry to startle you." His lips formed the words, revealing a gap-toothed smile.

Normally Cassie would have smiled back. Today she wasn't in the mood. "Mike Lawson didn't kill that man."

"I know."

"You know?" Even though she couldn't hear her own voice, she could feel its tremble. "If you know, why is he still in there? Why are they still asking him questions?"

"This isn't my case. It happened outside the Denver city limits. The county has jurisdiction. And they don't know Mike like you and I do. They have to go strictly by evidence."

"What evidence? His gun?"

Surprise widened Detective Grady's eyes.

Cassie almost clapped a hand over her mouth. She'd forgotten she wasn't supposed to know about the gun.

Tim Grady narrowed his eyes, studying her. "His service weapon was found at the scene. Yes."

"But Mike didn't even have the gun. It was stolen when he was beaten up. Wasn't that why he was suspended?"

"The sheriff's department can't just take Mike's word for that. Theoretically he could have reported it missing when he had it all along. In fact, I'm afraid that could make his situation worse."

"How?" She couldn't imagine things being worse than this. Or maybe she just didn't want to.

"It shows premeditation."

She shook her head. How could this be happening? This was getting out of hand. Way out of hand. "But I was with him at Kardascian's house. He was trying to save the man's life, not kill him. And I have no reason to lie. Why can't they take my word?"

"You were with him the entire time?"

She scanned through her memory. It had all happened so fast. It was all so unexpected. She'd been arguing with Mike about who was going to ask Kardascian about Nick Warner, about the "list," about the disk she was trying to decode. She'd thought Mike was exaggerating about the possible danger. She'd thought he and Evangeline were merely coddling the deaf girl.

But that was before Mike saw something in the garage. Before he'd ordered her to lock herself in the car and call 9-1-1. Before she'd gone looking for him and found him beside Kardascian…up to his elbows in blood.

"You weren't with him the entire time, were you?"

She stared at Grady's lips. She didn't want to say anything. She didn't want to admit it was true. "I was with him almost the entire time."

"But not the entire time."

Her shoulders slumped. "When I caught up with him, he was trying to save Mr. Kardascian's life. Doesn't that count?"

"Not good enough. Like I said, the county sheriff can't just take our word for it. They have to go by the evidence."

Evidence. Since Mike didn't kill Kardascian, there wasn't any evidence to find, right? And weren't people supposed to be innocent until proven guilty? "What kind of evidence do they need?"

"Enough to prove he had the means and opportunity to kill Milo Kardascian."

Cassie nodded. "The means, meaning the gun, right?"

"Right."

"And the opportunity?"

"The space of time that you weren't with

him. The time he and Kardascian were alone."

"He didn't do it." If she still had her hearing, she could swear she hadn't heard gun fire, but as things were she wasn't a lot of help. Still, there had to be something. "He had no reason to do it. Doesn't that count for anything?"

"Motive. It counts for a lot in court, even though it's not required to charge him."

"So go tell the county detective that Mike had no motive."

Detective Grady shook his head. "I can't do that."

"Why not? I thought you were his partner. His friend."

"I am. But it wouldn't be the truth."

Cassie stared at him. What was he trying to say? She tried to ask, tried to make her voice function, but it caught in her throat as if she'd forgotten how to speak.

"How well do you know Mike, Ms. Allen?"

Cassie chewed her bottom lip. She'd worked with him on a couple of cases. Flirted with him a little. Fantasized about him, certainly. She liked him, more than she felt comfortable with most of the time. But other than that, she supposed she knew very little about him. "Enough to know he's no murderer."

Grady nodded. "I believe that, too. But it's not that simple. Mike and Kardascian have a history."

Cassie didn't have to try very hard to remember the exchange between Evangeline and Mike when the millionaire CEO's picture flashed on the screen in the PPS boardroom. And on the drive to Kardascian's cabin, Mike had warned her the man had a brutal nature. And that he'd been in trouble with police. "What history?"

"Mike was called to Kardascian's house a few times. And his condo downtown. That was back before either one of us made detective."

"Mike told me about that." A sure sign he had nothing to hide. Right?

"The last call…Kardascian had beat up his girlfriend. Bad."

Cassie sucked in a breath despite her attempt to face whatever Detective Grady said with her utmost cool.

"It wasn't the first time. Milo Kardascian was kind of known for taking out his frustrations on whatever woman was attracted enough to his money to put up with him. That last call…" Detective Grady paused, as if he had to force himself to go on. "Mike crossed the line. He messed up Kardascian pretty good."

Cassie's head snapped back as if the words were a physical blow. She didn't know what she'd expected Grady to say, but it wasn't this. "Mike hit him?"

"Bastard deserved it. Didn't want to stop beating on the woman even for the police. So Mike stopped him." Tim's lips pulled back in a hint of a smile. The smile quickly faded. "Kardascian went after Mike, though. Called in political favors. Made Mike's life a living hell for a while. Almost drummed him off the force. Certainly slowed down his career. It's the only reason I made detective before Mike."

"That's why they think Mike killed him? Payback?"

The detective lifted a shoulder. "It's been known to happen."

Cassie shook her head. "They have to know Mike wouldn't do that. The rest of his record should speak for itself."

"Like I said, it comes down to evidence. Whether or not ballistics can prove Mike's service pistol is the murder weapon. Whether or not a powder residue test proves he recently fired it." He gave her a smile filled not with pity, but understanding. Maybe even sympathy. "I'm sure he'll appreciate that you believe in him, though."

She did believe in him. After what had happened with Kardascian, she even had a limited appreciation for his protective streak. If she had stumbled onto the millionaire's murder alone, who knew what could have happened? She might be in the morgue right now, beside the CEO. "He's always done a good job on the cases he worked with PPS."

"Sure." He gave her a grin suggesting he thought her belief in Mike went deeper than that.

She shifted uncomfortably. "He has done a good job. A very good job. Evangeline says he's one of the most honest cops in Denver. And after that Dirty Three scandal, I sometimes wonder if he's the last one left." She paused, realizing the implication of her words. "No offense. I know there are plenty of honest cops. I'm just frustrated."

"No offense taken." His smile widened to show the gap. "And I agree. Mike is an honest cop and I'm sure the evidence will show it."

She hoped so. She sure hoped so. For obvious reasons…and reasons she didn't want to examine too closely.

Chapter Five

"So, can I go?" Mike eyed the sheriff's detective, a guy named Abramson that he'd grown far too familiar with over the past several hours. Hell, he didn't even know how much time he'd spent staring at the government beige walls in this tiny box of an interview room, nothing but two chairs and a camera staring down at him from the corner. But however long he'd been here was too long. Much too long.

Abramson frowned down at the new report he'd just been handed. His eyebrows pulled together, forming a single bushy ridge topping his craggy features. "The preliminary ballistics examination shows your Sig Sauer is likely the murder weapon."

Mike took a deep breath, trying to quell his rising frustration. "I'm not saying it wasn't.

I just didn't fire it." Abramson had taken swabs of his forearms several hours before to test for gun-powder residue, evidence that he'd recently fired a gun. Since he hadn't, the test had to come back negative.

Provided this whole thing wasn't some sort of setup to do away with a traitor cop. For all he knew, Abramson could be drinking buddies with the Dirty Three. At the very least, he was a cop, and cops, as Mike's dad was fond of repeating, took care of their own. "What about the residue test?"

"The results aren't back yet."

"They're going to be negative. Your killer is out on the streets right now, covering up anything that leads to him. And all the while you're wasting time with me. And Cassie Allen."

Abramson leaned forward. "That's one thing I don't understand. How does Ms. Allen fit into all of this?"

Mike felt a hitch low in his gut. "She doesn't." He shouldn't have mentioned Cassie at all. Instead of convincing the county detective she had nothing to do with the case, all he'd done was show he was concerned about her. And if this was Mike's case, he'd do exactly what Abramson was doing—he'd try to exploit that concern to get answers.

"I'd like to believe that, Lawson. Ms. Allen seems like a nice woman. But I have yet to hear a good reason for her being at Kardascian's house. And until someone sheds some light on that, I'm afraid I'll have to keep asking questions."

Mike forced himself to refrain from rolling his eyes. "Ask away, but my answers are going to be the same ones I've been giving all day. I didn't kill Kardascian. I found him with a bullet hole in his chest, and I tried to save him. Why won't you listen to me?"

"I need the overtime."

Mike slumped back in his chair. Just what he needed, a detective who was even more fond of sarcasm than he was.

"Don't take this personally, Lawson. I think you're a great cop. Hell, I think you did the right thing, offing a bastard like Kardascian. The guy had it coming for a long time."

Mike couldn't agree more. But he knew enough not to admit it.

"Hell, if someone like Kardascian laid a hand on a little dish like Cassie Allen and

I had anything to say about it, I'd probably do the same thing."

"By the time Cassie saw Kardascian, he was dead."

"I didn't say he laid a hand on her today."

Mike's ears burned. He wanted nothing more than to set the detective straight. The thought of him implying Cassie…

"Yeah, if it was up to me, I'd give you a medal. A lifesaving award for taking Kardascian out of the way. But at least you get Cassie Allen's undying gratitude. That makes going through all this crap worth it, I bet."

He gritted his teeth, keeping his mouth firmly shut. Abramson was fishing. He could never tie Cassie to Kardascian, because the connection didn't exist. But if Mike showed he cared too much about her, Abramson would sure as hell connect Cassie to him. A connection that—if Abramson was pals with the Dirty Three—could bring her all sorts of trouble she didn't deserve.

He never should have taken Evangeline's assignment.

"When I think about what it would be like

to have her indebted to me, I can understand exactly why you'd take out Kardascian."

Mike grunted. "You should write fiction, Abramson."

"Come on. You can't tell me she isn't grateful for what you did."

"I escorted Cassie Allen to Kardascian's to discuss a case he's involved with at PPS. Anything beyond that is a figment of your imagination."

"You want to stick with that?"

"It's the truth."

"What if I tell you Cassie Allen is singing a very different story?"

Mike's gut bunched like a fist. Cassie hadn't made up something in a misguided effort to save him, had she? If she had, he needed to set things straight and he needed to set them straight now. "If she's saying she has anything to do with Kardascian or me, she's lying."

The county detective studied him through narrowed eyes. "Even if what she said saves your ass?"

Mike nodded. "Even then. She'd never seen Kardascian face-to-face until today. And all that's ever been between her and me is work. I headed up a Denver PD task force that worked with Evangeline Prescott on a couple of occasions, and Cassie is an employee of PPS. End of story."

"And you're sticking to that?"

"Yes."

"Your funeral."

A knock sounded.

Abramson ambled to the door. He opened it and a deputy handed him a report. He closed the door and paced across the floor of the small interview room, looking down at the paperwork in his hands.

The residue-test result. It had to be.

Mike waited. If someone in the sheriff's department had doctored the evidence against him, this would be the time to hit him with it. Abramson would use it like a club to try to pummel him into a confession.

Abramson kept walking, his club nowhere in sight.

Time for Mike to do a little pushing. "So what's next, Detective? Are you going to arrest me now, or am I free to go?"

Abramson kept pacing as if he hadn't heard.

"You can't prove the gun was in my possession or that it was fired by me. Your only witness says I was trying to save Karda-scian's life. You have nothing. Do I have to call a lawyer to pry me out of this place?"

Abramson stared at him for a full ten seconds without blinking. Twenty. Finally he shrugged his bony shoulders. "Yeah. Go. What the hell. I know where to find you."

Mike pushed to his feet, the muscles in his legs eager for the movement. "You don't have reason to hold Cassie Allen, either."

"She left a couple of hours ago."

A couple of hours? Good. He'd read Abramson right. All his talk was just that, talk. Designed to exploit any guilt Mike might be feeling, to press him into a corner. If he really believed there was any significance to the relationship between Mike and Cassie, he would have held her for questioning as long as he legally could.

"She was trying to convince us you're a saint."

Cassie? A warm shimmer loosened the unease in his gut. Since walking into the PPS offices this morning, he'd gotten the unmistak-able impression she didn't want him anywhere near her. It felt good that she believed in him after all.

He caught himself before the feeling went too far. "She doesn't know me very well."

Abramson shot him a droll look. "Apparently not. You can get your truck back tomorrow. If we're done with it by then. The handgun you had with you at Kardascian's might take a little longer." Abramson pulled open the door.

"Great." If losing his backup weapon and finding a ride back to the ranch were the biggest problems he faced after all this, he was lucky. He supposed he could always call the old man about the ride. Whether his father would choose to answer was anyone's guess.

"Stick around town," Abramson said. "I'm sure I'll have more questions for you."

"I know the drill." Mike stepped out of the room and walked down the short hall leading to the front vestibule. Relief filtered through his blood and penetrated his bones with each step. As long as Cassie wasn't dragged into this mess, he could deal with it. And the first thing he'd do—even before figuring out a way to get home without his truck—was to call Evangeline and demand she find Cassie a real bodyguard. One the Dirty Three and their supporters still on the job weren't gunning for.

With Abramson on his heels, Mike rounded the corner and pushed through the heavy door to the vestibule.

There standing in the entrance to the sheriff's department headquarters was Cassie. A smile of relief broke over her face that only a blind man could miss. She raised her hands. *I thought you might need a ride.*

CASSIE KEPT HER EYES on the road. The bad thing about preferring to sign instead of speak was that she couldn't carry on much of a conversation while driving.

That was the good thing, too.

Since they'd left the Jefferson County Sheriff's Department and gotten on Highway 58 out of Golden, Mike had been on a solid rant about the dangers of letting law enforcement know she had anything to do with him. From what she'd chosen to read from his lips and flying hands, she got the distinct impression he wanted to wrap her up in Bubble Wrap and pack her away for her own good.

Luckily, though it was late enough at night that the traffic was light, she had to focus on the road. An easy way to tune him out. And with her hands on the wheel, he certainly couldn't expect her to reply. But the urge to give him a return lecture about how she already had a doting, overprotective father and she didn't need him to fill that role pressed at her lips.

She took in a deep breath. The sweet smell of malt from the Coors brewery still filled the car's interior, almost drowning out the subtle scent of leather and male.

Almost.

She had to be crazy, going back to the sheriff's department to pick up Mike. Or maybe she was just a masochist. Whenever he was near, she felt like a helpless little kid. No, like a helpless, giddy teenager who couldn't control her hormones.

At least if he kept up this overprotective act, she'd have a constant reminder of why she couldn't throw herself into his arms. Nothing like being cast in the role of poor little deaf girl to quash the wayward libido.

Mike's light touch on her arm caused her to jump. She glanced at him.

Drive to your apartment, he signed.

He wanted to stay at her apartment? A tremor started somewhere south of her stomach. He couldn't be planning to watch over her twenty-four hours a day, could he? She shook her head and returned her focus to the road.

He tapped her arm again.

The only thing more disconcerting than his scent was his touch. She gave him another glance.

I have to swing by police headquarters, he signed. *Your apartment is near PPS, right?*

She let out a relieved breath and nodded, feeling as if she'd dodged a bullet. She exited the interstate and wound her way through surface streets. With traffic growing sparse in the late hour, it didn't take long to get to her apartment. A converted warehouse, her loft was in a square redbrick building adjacent to the downtown pedestrian mall. Full of life and energy. And an easy commute to PPS.

She pulled to the curb. Taking a deep breath, she twisted in her seat to face him. *Well, I'll see you tomorrow.*

To her relief, he nodded. *I'm sorry to have put you through all that at the sheriff's department.*

It's not as if it was your fault.

That depends on who you ask.

She knew he'd meant it as a joke. Sort of. But there was far too much truth in the statement to make her laugh. *The sheriff's department and Denver police don't really think you killed Milo Kardascian, do they?*

He twitched one shoulder in a shrug. *Some do. Some don't.*

It seemed like everyone we saw today did. Except your partner.

That's what partners are for.

And the rest?

They're doing their jobs.

She supposed that was a defense, but it seemed like a poor one to her. The people who worked with Mike should know him better than that. Here she'd only been around him a handful of times before today and she knew he was no murderer. He was a good man. Overprotective. Disconcerting. Not someone *she* needed to be around. But a good man nonetheless, despite any so-called "evidence" in his past. *Detective Grady explained some things to me.*

He narrowed his eyes on her, scanning her face. *Let me guess. My history with Kardascian.*

She nodded.

He stared out the windshield, his lips visible in the glow from a nearby streetlight.

"I should have told you…all of it…before we went to his house."

Why didn't you?

"I don't know. I was ashamed, I guess. It wasn't my finest moment." The muscle along his jaw flexed. The fine lines in the outer corners of his eyes dug deeper. "One in a string of many."

Her chest tightened. Unthinking, she reached out, cupping her hands over his.

He turned, his eyes finding hers. "What you did—trying to convince the county I was innocent, driving back to pick me up—you shouldn't have done it."

She frowned. He'd already harped on all the reasons she shouldn't have come back to the sheriff's department, all the ways any association with him could bring the spite of his enemies down on her head. But he was missing the point, the point he didn't want to hear. She couldn't have *not* done it. She couldn't have left him stranded.

"I guess all I'm saying is thanks for believing in me. It's been a while."

She didn't know what to say. *Why wouldn't I?*

One side of his mouth crooked upward. "Just thanks."

You're welcome. She glanced down at her fingers twined with his. Heat flushed across her cheeks. Pulling her hands away, she gestured to the redbrick building. *Well, this is my apartment, so...* She let the movement of her fingers trail off, hoping he would climb out of the car before this moment became even more awkward.

He glanced at the building then back to her. *I'll walk you to your apartment door.*

Her chest tightened further still. She needed to get away from him. The way she'd grabbed his hands without thinking proved that. She couldn't have him hovering over her, taking care of her, protecting her from the army of threats he saw around every corner. She needed space. She needed a normal life. She needed to not feel so out of control. *I've managed to live on my own for ten years now. Just like a normal person. I can manage one more night.*

His eyebrows shot upward. *Where did that come from? I'm not saying—*

Not saying what? That a deaf girl shouldn't

be living alone? That I might not be able to handle it?

He lowered his brows into a frown. *Cassie, you're being ridiculous. I'm not trying to coddle the deaf girl. But I'm also not leaving until you are safe inside your locked apartment. So we can sit here and sign back and forth, or you can let me walk you to the door.*

She grabbed the handle with a shaky hand and pushed the door open. He was right. She was being ridiculous. What was she afraid of? That Mike walking her to the door would make this a date? That he'd kiss her goodnight?

Or that she'd want him to?

She thrust herself out of the car and locked the doors with a flick of her remote. When she reached the curb, Mike was waiting. He followed her into the building and up the stairs without a word.

She led him to her apartment door and slipped her key into the lock. Letting the key chain dangle, she turned to face him. *Thanks. I'm glad you were with me at Kardascian's. Though I'm sorry it didn't work out so well for you.* She knew she was being overly formal, stiff, but she couldn't help it. She felt that if she let her guard down for just one second, she'd brush against him, or tilt her head back for a kiss or do something else to lead him on. Something else to humiliate herself.

It will be fine. They can't convict me without evidence.

She nodded. *Good night, then.* She stuck out her hand to shake. Her fingers trembled at the thought of touching his. God, she was lame.

Mike clasped her hand, engulfing her fingers in his warm palm. He pulled her close, giving her a minihug with the other arm that lasted about a second.

When he released her, she stood staring at him blankly. Her thoughts were so focused on the light contact between them she couldn't remember what she was supposed to do next.

I wasn't kidding. Safe behind the locked door or I'm not leaving. He gave her a warning smile.

Her thoughts clicked into place. Yes. Inside. Where she wouldn't have to worry about her insecurities, Mike's hovering, or making a fool of herself over a simple touch.

I'll see you tomorrow. She turned the key and pushed the door open.

For a moment, she wasn't sure what she was seeing. Papers were scattered on the area rug under her baby grand piano. Kitchen cupboards and drawers hung open, their contents spilling out. And the Native American pottery she kept on the credenza of her office were strewn across the wood floor, broken into shards.

Chapter Six

Mike grabbed Cassie's arm and pulled her out of the doorway. He reached for his weapon. His fingers hit air. Damn. Not a good time to be without a gun.

Cassie's wide eyes connected with his. *Is someone inside?*

He didn't know. And without a weapon, he had no business finding out. He flipped open his phone and punched in 9-1-1.

"Nine-one-one. What is your emergency?"

Compared to the race of his heartbeat and buzz of adrenaline in his body, the voice seemed almost unnaturally calm. "This is Detective Lawson. I have a break-in. The guy might still be here. I need officers ASAP." He gave Cassie's address to the dispatcher in a hushed voice, along with a few more details before he hung up.

He looked down at Cassie. *Are you okay?*

She shook her head.

He couldn't blame her. Her eyes were so wide, she looked as if she might be on the edge of going into shock. Not surprising after all she'd been through this morning. Now this. *How many rooms?*

What?

In your apartment. How many rooms?

Just the great room and the loft upstairs.

At least the floor plan was simple. Fewer places for someone to hide. In the glance he'd gotten when Cassie opened the door, he hadn't seen anyone in the great room. If anyone was still inside, he had to be in the loft. *Any other exit?*

There's a fire escape.

Does it reach up to the loft?

She nodded.

There was no way he could cover both the front entrance and the fire escape at the same time. And without a weapon...

A crash erupted from inside the room. The sound of glass breaking.

Flattening to the hallway wall, he inched around the edge of the door and peeked inside. If someone was coming, he wanted to know about it. He might not have a weapon, but that didn't prevent him from throwing himself on the guy to keep him away from Cassie. Whatever he had to do.

Cassie moved close behind him, trying to see inside herself.

He pushed her back with one hand. The last thing he needed was for her to do something stupidly heroic. He could conjure up enough stupid heroism for both of them.

Breath rasping in his ears, he scanned the apartment. He didn't see any movement, any glass that could have caused the sound. Then he spotted the window.

At first it looked as if the window itself was merely open. The blinds were pulled down and waving slightly, blown by a light breeze from outside. But as the blinds moved against the window, it tilted to the side, one side hitting glass and the other open air.

"He went out the window."

Cassie nodded, stepping forward as if she planned to race into the apartment to see for herself.

He reached out an arm to stop her. "Cassie. Stay here. Don't move. I'm going in. Do you understand?"

She nodded.

Mike moved cautiously into the apartment. He was pretty sure the place was empty. Almost certain. Still his gut tensed with each step across the hardwood floor, waiting for the sound of a trigger pulling, the force of a bullet slamming into his chest.

He crossed the room. He was halfway to the window when he heard the light hiss of Cassie's breath and shuffle of her shoes on the floor. Damn. He should have known she wouldn't stay put. He raised a hand, warning her back.

Her footfalls behind him slowed.

At least he could convince her to hesitate, if not listen to him completely. He reached the window. Lifting the edge of the blind, he peered outside.

The window was broken, just as he'd guessed. Half the pane was gone, cracks fanning out like a spiderweb spread across the rest of the glass. Shards crunched under Mike's boots. The window had broken into the apartment. As if someone was breaking in.

It didn't make sense. Whoever had ripped Cassie's place apart had spent a good long time on his handiwork. He certainly hadn't just broken in seconds ago.

Or had it been a mistake? Had he been sneaking out and slipped while closing the window?

Mike leaned toward the pane. A sound reached him from outside. The pluck of footsteps on steel. He peered through the window. Movement stirred on the fire escape. A dark figure. Man? Woman? He couldn't tell. The figure dropped to the sidewalk below. A streetlight glistened on dark hair.

Mike would never catch him. But he might be able to head him off.

He spun around. Slipping on glass shards, he almost went down before regaining his balance. He focused on Cassie, signing and saying his words at the same time. "Stay here and wait for police." He raced past her and sprinted for the door. If he could reach the street before the burglar disappeared into a car or blended with people milling on the pedestrian mall, he might have a shot at identifying him.

He dashed down the stairs, his feet thunking each step hard enough to send shock waves up his legs. He leaped over the last few steps and pushed out the door.

The night outside was cool and crisp and few people dotted the sidewalks and pedestrian mall. Good. That would make finding the dark-haired burglar easier. Mike set out down the sidewalk toward the direction the burglar had been heading. As he reached the corner, he heard the apartment building's door open behind him.

Cassie.

Damn. The woman didn't listen and it had nothing to do with her inability to hear. At least she was still half a block behind him. Even if he ran smack into whoever had broken into her apartment, she would be far enough behind to be safe.

Or so he hoped.

Where the hell were those police sirens? There had to be officers downtown. So where were they?

He rounded the corner, bracing a hand on the brick to keep his balance without slowing down.

A silhouette moved out of the shadow a block away. Dark hair, dark clothing. That had to be him. A car idled near the curb.

Mike's breath roared in his ears. His heart felt as if it would pound right through his ribs. He pushed his legs to move faster. He still had half a block to go.

The dark figure ran to the car and ducked inside. He closed the door behind him as the car pulled out and roared toward him.

Mike screeched to a halt. He focused on the car, a dark sedan. Maybe an older Taurus. He scanned the bumper. No license plate.

The car drew closer. The passenger window inched down.

Holy hell. Mike's gut clenched and rose into the vicinity of his throat. He needed to find cover. If the guy had a gun, he was a goner.

He raced for the curb and ducked behind a parked minivan.

The sedan drove past. No shots fired. Nothing. It moved slowly past him and continued down the street.

Mike followed its movement toward the corner. Cassie popped out from around the building, following the path he'd just taken. Her hair glowed like darkened flame in the streetlights. Her pale cheeks flushed pink from exertion.

The sedan continued its slow approach. Its window lowered farther. The barrel of a gun poked through the open space.

Rising to his feet, Mike launched into a dead run. How could he have been so stupid? How could he have thought she'd be safe?

His muscles burned. His feet stung as they slapped the concrete. He yelled, his message more bellow than words.

Cassie watched him, a confused look on her face. She slowed her steps but kept moving toward him. Toward the sedan.

The crack of gunfire split the air.

Chapter Seven

Cassie froze, staring at the small puff of dust exploding from the brick six inches from her head. What in the world? She looked to Mike, watching him race toward her. Fast, yet in slow motion. She couldn't move. Couldn't think. She just watched, unable to process what was going on.

Mike grabbed her arm. He pulled her toward the cars parked along the curb. He yanked her to the ground.

Her knees hit concrete, the force shuddering up her spine. She felt a sound stir in her chest, the vibration of a scream.

Mike came down on top of her. The weight of his body pressed her flat to the sidewalk, making breath whoosh from her lungs.

Gunfire. That's what it was. Someone was

shooting at them from the car. Someone was trying to kill them. Trying to kill her.

Heat shot through her, followed by cold. A chill that burrowed into her bones, making her shake from the inside out. Face against concrete, she couldn't see anything. She couldn't tell what was going on. Were they still shooting? Had the car stopped? Circled back? She struggled to raise her head, to see something, anything in the darkness.

Mike shifted his weight, pressing her more securely to the ground.

Second ticked after second, passing as slowly as hours. Were they still shooting? She didn't know. Damn this silence in her head. If she'd been able to hear the shots, she would have known what was happening. She would have been able to react.

If Mike hadn't pulled her down, she would be dead.

A scream welled in her throat. She pushed it back. Pushed it down. She had to remain calm. She had to be strong. Whatever happened, she had to stay in control.

Finally Mike moved his head. A heartbeat later he lifted his weight off her. Gripping her arm in one hand, he pulled her up.

Her legs shook. Her muscles sagged, about as able to support her weight as jelly.

Mike slipped an arm around her back, under her armpits. Half dragging and half carrying her, he guided her around the corner of the building and to the front entrance. He pulled on the door. Locked.

And her keys were in her purse, which she'd dropped in the hall outside her apartment.

It wasn't hard to read Mike's lips, even in the dark. "Damn, damn, damn. Where are those sirens? Where are the freaking sirens?"

Cassie forced herself to stand upright, to move, to think. She stepped to the doorbell panel next to the front door and started punching buttons. She couldn't hear if anyone answered. She just hoped one of her neighbors would buzz the door open without even finding out who was outside.

Maybe the same way whoever had wrecked her pottery had gotten in.

Mike leaned over the intercom. He pushed the button. "This is Detective Mike Lawson of the Denver Police Department. I need you to open the door." He hesitated for a second, then scowled.

Apparently whoever had answered did not want to let a police officer inside. Cassie pushed the button. "I'm Cassie Allen. I live in apartment Three B. Please, buzz us in."

Another scowl from Mike.

Even she wasn't welcome in her own building.

Mike's head jerked around. Cassie followed his line of vision.

A dark sedan turned down the street and headed straight toward them.

Her stomach lurched into her throat. She was going to be sick. All over the sidewalk. Whoever was in that car could just mow her down while she was on her knees retching.

Mike grabbed her arm and pulled her out of the doorway and down the sidewalk away from the approaching car.

She willed her stomach to stay calm. She forced her legs to function, to hold her weight, to match Mike stride for stride. They raced down the sidewalk.

The car drew closer. She could feel it, dark like an ominous force. She braced herself for the puff of dust that signaled a bullet pinging off the brick.

Or worse, the pain of lead digging into flesh.

They reached the side of the building that flanked the pedestrian mall, weaving around planters and the smattering of people. Partway down the block, Mike pulled her into a darkened doorway and pushed her down to the ground. He crouched in front of her, shielding her with his body.

Tears pressed at the back of her eyes and fuzzed the edge of her vision. She struggled to pull one dusty breath after another into her lungs. She had to hold it together. As frightened as she was, she couldn't lose control.

Outside the doorway, the sedan's dark outline crept down the cross street, hunting, stalking. It paused in clear view of the doorway.

She took in a breath and held it. She pressed closer to Mike, praying that they blended with the darkness. Seconds ticked by. Questions raced through her mind. Had they been spotted?

Finally, slowly, the car continued down the street.

Thank you, God.

She let out the breath and scooped dusty air into her starving lungs. The tremble in her chest grew and expanded until it claimed her whole body.

Mike squeezed her to him, then released and searched her eyes. His face was flushed behind the bruises, the muscles in his jaw and neck tight. "Are you okay?"

Okay? She was far from okay. She doubted she'd ever be okay again. She nodded.

"I'm so sorry about that. God, I'm so sorry."

Sorry? What was he talking about? She opened her mouth to answer. She wanted to speak out loud, speak so he could hear her, but her voice caught in her throat. *You saved my life,* she signed with fingers shaking so badly they had to be nearly impossible to read.

"You never should have been in danger in the first place. If I hadn't been so bullheaded, so set on nailing the person who tossed your apartment, you wouldn't have come so close to…" He dropped his focus to the floor.

She shook her head and cleared her throat. "You saved my life, Mike."

She didn't know if it was the timbre of her voice, the raw emotion that threatened to choke her, or just the way she'd said his name, but he raised his eyes and met hers.

She could feel the hot rush of tears stream-ing down her face. She could feel the grip on her emotions disintegrating. She couldn't do anything to stop any of it. A sob bubbled from her lips. Then another. Soon she was gasping for breath, drowning in a flood of emotion.

Mike tightened his arm, pulling her to his shoulder. "It's okay. We're alive. We're okay." He kissed her forehead, her cheeks, her lips.

She kissed him back. Over and over. Unable to stop. She clung to him, vulnerable, weak, everything she didn't want to be. Everything she promised herself she'd never give into. But she couldn't do anything to stop it. All she wanted at that moment was to have Mike's arms around her. All she wanted was for him to take care of her and she didn't care about the consequences.

God help her.

"THE DENVER PD NEVER SHOWED." Mike watched the faces of the two Prescott Personal Securities agents Evangeline had sent to Cassie's apartment. The two agents were about as different as night and day.

The woman, Mike knew. Lily Clark, a little blond pixie with a spontaneous streak who, until recently, had worked as a police officer with the Denver PD. He'd always liked Lily, though at times she seemed too smart for her own good. Still, she'd been a good officer, and he had to admit it was nice to have a former cop around to help him talk this out.

The other, Cameron Morgan, was built as if he could play for the Denver Broncos. Even taller than Mike's six foot one, Cameron was ex-military and it showed in the way he carried his body. Tense and ready. As if at any given time, he was ready to either go out for a pass or jump from a helicopter.

"How did you get back here?"

Mike exchanged looks with Cassie. The salty taste of her tears still clung to his lips. He didn't have to close his eyes to remember the shudder of her sobs against his chest.

She was the first to look away. She signed slowly, Mike filling in the gaps verbally when the agents didn't understand. *We waited until the car passed and doubled back. A neighbor finally let us back into the building.*

Lily nodded. "I can poke around, find out why the police didn't show."

"I know why they didn't show. Because it

was me who called." A cop's biggest nightmare. Calling for backup and being hung out to dry. "I should have seen it coming. I betrayed the brotherhood, they betrayed me right back."

Lily shook her head. "You took down some dirty cops. Just three criminals in a whole department of good cops. It was your duty."

"That's not the way they see it. Even my old man thinks I should have handled the Dirty Three differently, that I should have cleaned things up quietly from the inside, not gone public. He would probably agree that I deserved this tonight. But Cassie didn't." The fear that had gripped Mike's chest when he'd seen the gun barrel poke through the open window had turned to a vaguely nauseous unease. But the memory hadn't faded. The shooter hadn't fired at him. He'd gone straight for Cassie. "I guess Evangeline was right about that disk being important."

Cameron glanced around the wreckage of Cassie's apartment. "I guess so."

"And that's why we're here," Lily said. She started unpacking the equipment cases she and Cameron had brought with them. "First, we're going to dust for prints. If we can identify whoever trashed this place, we have our shooter, right? Or at least someone who is working with our shooter."

Mike helped unpack the metallic powder and magnetic applicators, clear tape and white cards that made up the fingerprinting kit. "I can probably talk my partner into running these through AFIS." Grady had only to flash that goofy smile and Lois, the print analyst, would run anything he wanted through the Automated Fingerprint Identification System.

"Good. If you have problems, let me know," Lily said. "I still have some favors to collect."

"And Evangeline has contacts none of us even know about." Cameron lifted a series of cameras and small microphones out of their cases and arranged them on the table.

You're wiring my apartment? Cassie signed, gesturing at the devices.

Cameron nodded. "I know Pinto is the expert when it comes to setting this stuff up. But he's on assignment, so you get me."

I've seen you do a pretty darn good job of setting up the tech equipment, Cam, Cassie signed.

Cameron dipped his head. "Thanks. I try. I'm going to be in the surveillance van outside tonight. If they come back, we'll be ready. Lenny has some great toys here that he just developed."

Glad to help test them. Cassie smiled, but the curve of her lips was shaky at best. *I'll help you set them up.*

Mike focused on the fingerprint kit. He wanted nothing more than to wrap Cassie in his arms and whisk her off to somewhere far away. Someplace where he could keep her safe, take care of her. Someplace where he didn't need backup.

While Cassie and Cameron planted cameras and microphones throughout the apartment, Lily and Mike dusted metallic powder onto the surfaces the intruder had likely touched. Using the clear tape, they lifted the prints they found and affixed them to white cards. When Cassie had finished helping Cameron with the equipment, Mike inked her fingers and rolled her fingers on cards of their own. Once they had eliminated Cassie's prints from the fingerprints they collected, those left were possibly the intruder's.

Cameron packed up the remainder of the

equipment. Strapping the cases over his broad shoulders, he stepped to the door. "I'll get set up outside. We should be live in fifteen minutes or so." He shut the door with a bang.

Cassie finished washing the ink from her hands. Fetching a broom and dustpan from a closet, she moved to the far side of the room and started sweeping up the glass from the broken window.

Mike checked to see that she wasn't watching before he approached Lily. "Are you staying with Cassie?"

The blonde looked up from the table where she was packing up the fingerprint-lifting supplies. "I'm going to another assignment."

"Cassie can't stay here by herself."

She frowned up at him. "Aren't you staying?"

Him?

The memory of the moments in the doorway shimmered through his blood. He wanted to stay. Too much. And that was precisely why he shouldn't. "I don't know if that's such a good idea."

Across the room, Cassie had moved to her office area and the pieces of pottery littering the floor.

"Why not? With Cameron out front, you don't need to worry about whether our brothers in blue are going to jerk you around. Oh, and there's this." Lily dipped a hand into one of the cases she'd carried up and pulled out a Glock, a holster and two boxes of ammunition. "We heard you lost both of your pieces."

He picked up the weapon and checked the breech. "Thanks."

"You don't sound convinced."

How could he explain how he'd felt holding Cassie in his arms in the doorway? How could he say that he liked her too much to be the one she relied on? The one who might just let her down?

"Convinced of what?" The mellow tones of Cassie's voice came from behind him.

He turned to look at her. He'd never walked away from anything in his life, but he needed to walk away now. Didn't he? He pictured himself walking to the door, opening it, stepping out and keeping going. He imagined lying in his bed back at the ranch, not knowing what was happening to Cassie, not knowing what danger she faced, not knowing if she was crying or frightened or about to do something brave and completely stupid. "Whether I'll ever be a cop again."

"You're going to quit the police force?"

Strangely enough, he could imagine that more easily than he could imagine walking away from Cassie right now. "I don't know. I was just thinking out loud."

Lily nodded. "Well, that's all for me. I'll tell Cam it's a go. And I'll see the two of you at the office tomorrow."

CASSIE EYED the cameras and microphones she'd helped Cameron place in strategic parts of the apartment. Cameron would be able to see nearly everything she and Mike did, hear everything they said. If it weren't for the fact that she'd almost been killed just a few hours before, she'd feel as if she was part of a TV reality series.

But that wasn't what was freaking her out. The thing that had her insides twitching was the prospect of Mike spending the night. Spending the night after what had happened between them.

Grabbing two glasses, she stuffed them into the cupboard, clinking them against the other glasses despite efforts to keep her hands steady.

She was being ridiculous, behaving like that hormone-driven teenager, but she couldn't help it. She wasn't used to being weak in front of other people. She wasn't used to falling apart. And she certainly wasn't used to desperately throwing herself at a man. Even if it was during life-threatening circumstances.

Of course, she wasn't exactly used to life-threatening circumstances, either.

And now she didn't know if it was just her, or if it was the kiss they'd shared that charged the air between them. But whatever it was, she had to deal with it. She had to put it aside and go back to being strong, being comfortable, being herself. She couldn't go through the night feeling this out of control.

At least if she and Mike signed, Cam probably wouldn't be able to understand most of what they were talking about.

Picking up the last of the dishes from the floor, she crossed to the center of the room where Mike crouched on the floor, collecting the papers strewn on the area rug under her piano. Taking a deep breath, she lowered herself to the floor near him and shuffled some papers together. She'd better get this over with. *I'm sorry. About earlier.*

Mike looked up from his stack of papers. *About what? Getting upset? I think you have a right after all that's happened.*

If only that's all she'd done. *About everything.*

He gave her an understanding smile. *You're not used to losing control, are you?*

Not used to it? She never lost control. She certainly wasn't weak and desperate. Not in front of others. *No. I can't afford to.*

Because you're deaf.

Because people are always waiting for me to be weak. For me to give them an excuse to take care of me.

People?

My parents, I guess. And my brother.

He lowered his eyebrows as if he disapproved.

She waved her hands, trying to erase the impression she'd given. *It's not like you think. They care about me. It's just that they were with me when it happened.*

When you lost your hearing?

She nodded. She didn't like thinking about

that day. Even now the whole thing felt surreal. As if it hadn't happened to her. As if it couldn't have.

How did it happen?

She took a deep breath. She didn't want to remember, didn't want to talk about it. But the way Mike was watching her—no pity in his eyes, just a calm question—the memory didn't seem so scary this time. For the first time since it had happened, she felt that maybe she could talk about it. *I was in college, living in the dorm. And I just woke up one morning with dizziness and a whooshing sound in my ear.*

Did you have it checked out?

Oh, yeah. I thought it was a cold at first or a sinus infection. My mom picked me up at the dorm and took me to the doctor. They put me through a ton of tests and an MRI, but they didn't find anything. Finally they guessed a virus of some kind had led to me developing something they call Sudden Sensorineural Hearing Loss. Really, they didn't know what caused it. She shrugged and gave him a smile. *But I guess I'm a rarity.*

He returned the gesture, the corners of his dark eyes crinkling and making him look more like a rugged cowboy than a city police detective. *I could have told you that.*

Smart ass.

A chuckle shook his chest. *So how are you a rarity?*

Sudden Sensorineural Hearing Loss usually only affects one ear. For me, it was both. She gave another shrug. *Just lucky, I guess.*

Yeah, lucky. His smile faded. *My brother was born deaf.*

That's tough. At least I could hear for my first twenty years.

He shook his head. *It wasn't like that. He didn't really understand what he was missing. I think it would be harder to know what it was like to hear and lose it.*

Maybe he had a point. She hadn't looked at it that way before. *It was tough at first. Especially with my family hovering over me. And my boyfriend...*

Your boyfriend? Mike prodded.

She shook her head. *It ended shortly after I became deaf.*

Mike's brows dipped. *He had a problem with it?* He leaned forward as if he was ready to scramble to his feet and beat the crap out of the guy.

She held up her hands and tried not to acknowledge the pleasure she felt at his reaction. *He felt sorry for me and tried to take care of me, is all. Well, he tried to take care of me a little too much. Made me feel I had suddenly become his poor invalid sister instead of his girlfriend.*

Stupid guy.

Cassie shifted. It suddenly felt awkward and uncomfortable sitting on the floor like this. She climbed to her feet, carrying the stack of papers with her. Tapping them into order on the corner of the baby grand, she arranged them in a pile before returning her gaze to Mike. *I didn't know you have a deaf brother. I guess that's why you know sign language so well.*

He lifted himself off the floor and added his stack of papers to hers. *I grew up with it.*

I'll bet you also grew up watching him deal with well-meaning people who tried to coddle him.

Mike shifted his feet on the floor. *Do you play?* He gestured at the baby grand piano.

Cassie tilted her head. She could have gotten whiplash from that rapid change of subject. But she supposed it was natural for

Mike to want to avoid talking about coddling his brother. As much as he seemed to understand where she was coming from, Mike took the promise to serve and protect to heart. She'd rarely met someone as protective as he was. She would be willing to bet he'd hovered over his brother as much as her family had hovered over her.

The piano, do you play? Mike repeated, as if he thought she hadn't understood the question.

She nodded. She couldn't count the number of times she'd been asked why she had a piano in her living room. After all, she was deaf. She couldn't enjoy music anymore, right? The piano movers alone had discussed it for at least an hour while trying to negotiate lifting it to the third floor. But she didn't think anyone had ever asked her if she played. *I was working on a minor in music before I lost my hearing.*

Do you still play? he signed.

His question caused a hitch under her breastbone. The fact that he wanted to know, that he seemed to think it was perfectly natural for her to play, touched her far more than it probably should. *Every day.*

Will you play for me?

The hitch turned to a tremble. She hadn't played for another living soul for years. Not since she'd awakened with the tinnitus in her ears. Not since she'd been pronounced permanently deaf.

He reached out and cleared the papers from the top of the piano. *Please?*

Cam will hear, she signed.

So you're afraid he doesn't like music, or you don't play for audiences? He crossed to her office area and set the stack of papers on her desk.

She used to love playing for audiences. But could she do it now? *I don't know what it will sound like.*

There's only one way to find out.

She took in a deep breath. She stepped to the piano and sank down on the bench. Closing her eyes, she fitted her fingers to the keys.

Lifting her fingers in the form she'd worked on perfecting since she was four years old, she launched into Rachmaninoff's *Rhapsody on a Theme of Paganini,* Variation XVIII, one of her favorites from when she'd discovered it in the movie *Somewhere In*

Time. She'd learned to play it in high school, the perfect vehicle to pour out the turmoil and drama of life as a teenager.

She didn't know if the longing she used to hear in the music was there anymore. The soaring passion. The exquisite pain. But she could imagine it. Shimmering in the vibration she felt through the air, through the keys. She could feel it in her chest. Stirring deep and sharp. Delicious and bittersweet.

After all that had changed in her life since that morning in college, the piano had remained. It still emoted for her. Still centered her. Still completed her. Even if she could no longer truly hear a note she played.

When she finished the piece, she left her hands on the keys, drinking in the last of the vibrations through her fingertips. Goose bumps rose on her arms, her legs. She left her eyes closed. To savor the moment…and because she was afraid to open them. Afraid to look into Mike's eyes. Afraid of what she'd see.

The bench shifted as he sat down beside her. His body heat warmed her. His scent, fresh and distinctive, teased the air around her. She drew in a deep breath.

If she saw pity in his eyes, she'd die. Or

that protective, coddling look. The look she knew too well. The look that made her feel weak and powerless.

The look that made her feel *less*.

A gentle fingertip brushed over her skin, pushing her hair back, tucking it behind her ear.

She swallowed into a tight throat and opened her eyes.

Mike watched her, a serious expression on his face, a sincerity glowing from his eyes that couldn't be faked. "That was beautiful."

She watched his lips curve around the words. Slowly. Deliberately. No pity. No coddling. A longing built in her chest, sharper than that in the music. She dropped her gaze to her fingers, still poised on the piano keys. "Thank you."

He slipped an arm around her, his hand cupping the point of her hip. His warmth enveloped her. His scent caressed her.

She didn't know what he was thinking, but she wanted to believe he was feeling the longing, too. Not longing for a kiss or a touch. Not feeling the electricity of attraction between them, although it was there. It was always there. But what lodged in her chest was more than that. The longing for a connection. An understanding. A mutual respect. She wanted to think he needed those things as much as she did. And that, against all odds, those things were possible to attain.

Even for her.

Chapter Eight

Mike didn't have a clue how he'd managed to spend the night under the same roof as Cassie and not kiss her again. And more. But somehow, he'd done it. Maybe it was knowing Cameron Morgan was watching and listening to their every move. Or maybe it had more to do with the realization that he wasn't the man she needed. And that he never could be.

He ran a hand over his face and levered himself off the great-room couch. He'd taken this assignment with the hope of somehow making up for not being there for Tommy. As if he could substitute one deaf person for another. What an idiot he was. Cassie was her own person. She had her own needs. Needs he could never fill.

And Tommy? He'd never make up for what he'd done to Tommy.

The hiss of a shower came from the loft's bathroom. Cassie getting ready for work. Ready to face her next challenge, despite all she'd been through in the past twenty-four hours.

Taking the downstairs bathroom, he turned on the shower, as well, and grabbed the shaving kit and extra clothing Lily and Cameron had brought him so he didn't have to stop back at the ranch. Pausing before hopping in the shower, he stared at his face in the mirror. His purple bruises were beginning to turn yellow around the edges, beginning to heal. If only deeper hurts would fade like that. Too bad those injuries never healed. The only thing he could do was make sure they didn't happen in the first place.

After he and Cassie had showered and dressed, they grabbed some toast and coffee and left Cameron's cameras to keep an eye on the apartment. The drive to the PPS offices was a short one and soon Cassie was back working on her computer and Mike was taking the familiar path to Revell's Gym, the place Grady, and many other cops, worked out at every morning without fail.

A healthier way of dealing with stress than drinking, that was for sure.

He almost changed his mind about that when he found his partner gliding up and down on the leg press, his face so flushed he looked like a heart attack waiting to happen. "You might want to take it easy, Grady. You look like you're about to bust a blood vessel."

Grady crouched low enough to take the weight from his shoulders. "What's up, Lawson?" Slipping off the machine, he glanced around the gym.

"Afraid to be seen with me?"

As if satisfied no one important was watching, Grady focused on Mike. "You're not the most popular guy around here. That's for sure."

That was the reason he'd wanted to head Grady off at the gym. "I figured this was a better place to catch you than your cubicle at headquarters."

"Thanks. I appreciate it. I don't need more headaches."

Guilt pricked the back of Mike's neck. He knew Grady was walking a fine line. As Mike's partner, he was probably an inch away from becoming a pariah by association. And with the emotional and financial stress of his wife's illness and death, Grady sure didn't need trouble on the job. "You been having a rough time of it?"

Grady shrugged a sweat-glistened shoulder. "There were a lot of cops who thought you did the right thing, turning in the Dirty Three. But others…"

"And now?"

"This business about Kardascian getting shot by your gun…it's rough."

"I didn't shoot him."

Grady waved a hand as if erasing Mike's statement from the air. "No kidding. It just doesn't look good, that's all. There are a lot of nervous people in the investigative division."

"Sorry, man. You one of them?"

"Me? Nothing makes me nervous. I'm the most laid-back cop on the job." He gave Mike a gap-toothed grin, as if to prove his point.

Mike considered the scene yesterday at Kardascian's cabin. "The lieutenant's nervous, isn't he?"

"Let's just say you might not be getting a Christmas card from him this year." Grady stepped past Mike and plunked down on an inclined ab board. Hooking his knees, he lay on the board, looking at Mike upside down. "Now what's up?"

"I need a couple of favors."

Grady lifted his body in a half sit-up. Lowering his shoulders back to the board, he hummed something through his nose that sounded like either a hem or a haw. "What kind of favors?"

"First, I need to know what officers were covering downtown during the evening shift."

"Last night?"

Mike nodded.

"Why? Something happen last night?"

"Someone broke into Cassie Allen's apartment. The suspect was still there when we arrived. He took a shot at her."

Grady paused mid-crunch. "She okay?"

"She was pretty shaken, but she's okay. She's a strong woman."

"I'll say. You should have seen her fighting for you at the Jefferson County Sheriff's Department yesterday."

Mike could imagine. He still worried that would come back to haunt her. And with the Denver PD's failure last night, maybe it had.

Grady lowered his shoulders back to the board. "So why do you want to know who was on that shift? Who responded to the call?"

"That's just it. No one responded."

"You gotta be kidding."

"Nope."

"Who called nine-one-one? You?"

Mike nodded.

"And you told them the intruder was still there?"

"Of course."

Grady stared at him, his face growing more and more pink as blood ran to his head. Finally he sat up and unhooked his legs from the board. He pivoted to face Mike and perched on the incline. "Okay. I'll poke around, find out who was on that shift, see if any report was filed on the incident."

"Appreciate it. Another thing."

The cautious look passed over Grady's face again. "Yeah?"

"I lifted some fingerprints from Cassie's apartment."

Grady shoved himself up from the ab board, picked up a set of dumbbells and started curling. "Let me guess. You want me to get someone at the lab to run them for you."

"Lois has a crush on you. She'll do anything you ask."

"But I'll have to give her something in return. You think that kind of special treatment is free?"

"So take her to dinner." He knew he probably shouldn't be pushing Grady into dating. His wife had only been gone six months. And, of course, Mike's motives were purely self-serving. But he needed those prints run. "Take her someplace expensive. On me."

"I was planning to spend some time at my cabin."

Mike nodded. He knew Grady enjoyed spending time at his little cabin in the mountains. He also knew this wasn't about Grady losing his quiet time. "You can go to the cabin any weekend. Take a chance. It's only dinner."

"I don't know if I'm ready for something like that."

"Throw in a movie or a show after dinner. Whatever she wants."

"How about a date for her besides me?"

"Oh, come on. You'll have a good time. It'll be good for you. And Lois is great."

"Right. Says the guy who's been spending all his time with Cassie Allen. I'll trade you."

Mike knew Grady was kidding, trying to take the focus off the painful reason for his return to the dating scene. But he still felt a pang of something in his chest. Something disturbingly close to possessiveness. "So will you ask Lois to run the prints?"

Grady hesitated for a second. "Yeah, sure, why not?"

"Thanks, man."

"Just call me Grady the sap."

"Always do."

Grady gave him a comical frown. "Anything else you need me to endanger my career or virtue for?" Grady pumped the dumbbells up and down, no doubt trying to work out some of the stress Mike was heaping on him. Sweat soaked his muscle shirt.

Mike was asking a lot. He knew it. If he could do something different, avoid putting his partner in this situation, he would. But if he was going to do the right thing, if he was going to come through for Cassie, he didn't have much of a choice. "Don't worry. I'll make it up to you."

"Don't you worry, Mikey. I'll make sure of it."

CASSIE ROLLED her shoulders. They'd started growing stiff hours ago. Now a deep ache had taken permanent residence at the back of her neck. But as much as her body was hurting due to staying in one spot all day, she couldn't take a break. Not now when she almost had it.

Or at least, she hoped.

She stared at the monitor, waiting for the computer to finish testing the last set of algorithms. The one that just had to contain the cipher she was looking for.

A hand tapped her shoulder.

Adrenaline lurched through her body. She spun around in her chair.

Sorry to startle you. Mike gave her a sheepish smile.

She shook her head. *I was just concentrating.*

On what? He leaned forward, trying to get a look at the monitor.

I'm waiting to see if this works. A chuckle escaped her lips. She couldn't help laughing at herself. She probably sounded like a ditz. Well, wasn't she? It wasn't as if staring at the monitor would make the computer run faster. *I guess I'm trying to will it to happen.*

If anyone can do that, it's you.

Warmth flushed through her at the sincere look in his eyes. She turned away, focusing on the screen. Unfortunately she couldn't sign without looking at Mike. "I wish I could will my brain to know the cipher they used on this disk."

She saw Mike smile out of the corner of her eye. "What?"

He held up his hands.

She swiveled to look at him full on. "What are you smiling about?"

"Nothing much. I was just surprised that you're talking."

She pressed her lips shut and lifted her hands from the keyboard. *Does it sound weird? Maybe I should go back to signing.*

"No. Talk. I love the sound of your voice. I told you, it's sexy."

A warm tremor fluttered high in her stomach. Her subconscious was definitely out to sabotage her. That's probably why she'd wanted to speak out loud. He'd mentioned before that her voice sounded sexy. Of course, since their kisses, seeing his lips curve around the word conjured images, tastes and sensations. Not somewhere she should be allowing her thoughts to go. *Maybe this isn't such a good—*

He turned his head before she could finish her statement and focused on the monitor. His brows gathered in a confused frown. "What exactly do you mean by a cipher?"

She followed his gaze to the monitor and let out a relieved breath. She could focus on decryption. She was comfortable with that, secure. She could talk about her work in her sleep. "To encrypt a disk, you apply a cipher to whatever data you're trying to limit access to. Simple ciphers could be things like substituting numbers for letters or interchanging letters in the alphabet. More complex ciphers work according to sophisticated computer algorithms that rearrange data bits."

"Let me guess, whoever recorded data on this disk used a complex cipher."

"You win a prize. Of course, if I had the decryption key, this would be simple."

"Decryption key?" He shook his head. "I sound totally clue free, don't I?"

"A decryption key is an algorithm that undoes the work of the encryption algorithm."

"Now you really lost me with that algorithm stuff."

"Algorithm stuff? Let me guess, you didn't like math class in school."

"I got lost in the forest of basic algebra and never found my way out. Even though I left bread crumbs."

She giggled. Oh, Lord, she was flirting. She took a deep breath. She'd have to put a clamp on that impulse. And fast. "I won't go into the particulars, then."

"Thank you."

"But the basic concept isn't that tough to understand." She fell back into the comfortable groove of teacher mode. At least if she focused on explaining the concepts behind cold hard numbers, she could keep from making a giggling fool of herself. "To encrypt data, you basically apply your key to the data. So if I'm using a key of the number four and I want to encrypt the number fifteen, I add the number four to the one and to the number five."

"Giving you fifty-nine."

"Right. Of course, that's a little simpler

than what I'm working with, but you get the idea."

"A little simpler?"

"Okay, a lot simpler." She shot him a wry smile, careful not to let her gaze rest too long.

"So the key you're talking about is a complex algorithm. At the risk of exposing just how ignorant I am, what exactly is an algorithm?"

"An algorithm is a formula for solving a problem."

"A mathematical formula?"

"Yes. So instead of applying a single number to change the message, whoever encrypted this message applied a complex mathematical formula. I have to find the formula that undoes the encrypting formula."

"More complicated than I'd even imagined. No wonder you have to use a computer to find this key."

"Even with a computer, I have to run an amazing number of ciphers to find the right one. An almost infinite number, possibly. It can take a while."

"How long?"

She focused on the monitor. The computer had finished running the last set of algorithms, but numbers still swam before her tired eyes. Not a list of any kind. Just several rows of numbers. And here she was sure this set was the charm. The ache at the back of her neck spasmed and spread between her shoulder blades. "At this rate, forever. I must not have the right key. I was sure this algorithm was the one. But all I'm getting are numbers."

Mike bent forward. His head near hers, he squinted at the screen. "What if that's what they encrypted? What if they're trying to hide numbers?"

Cassie turned to stare at him. Of course. Why hadn't she considered that? Her brain must be too tired. Or the trauma of the day before had made it short-circuit. "Jack thought the list might have something to do with names of investors."

"Could be. Or records of money laundering or illegal profits. Maybe offshore accounts and these numbers could be amounts. There are a lot of possibilities."

"It might be worth killing to keep that quiet." She shuddered slightly at the thought of who they were trying to kill—her. "So the list Nick Warner mentioned might be a list of bank accounts? Bank accounts set up by Mitchell

Caruthers, maybe? Maybe he did more than invest in TCM stock with his embezzled money. Maybe he did something illegal."

"Maybe. Except that all the money he embezzled was accounted for."

She considered this. "Maybe there's money we don't know about."

Mike shrugged. "But there's no evidence Caruthers was working with anyone. And seeing that he's dead, I don't see how he could have shot Kardascian."

"Maybe it has nothing to do with Caruthers or Nick Warner. We don't really know where this disk came from."

"True," Mike said. "But I don't believe in coincidence."

Neither did she. Frustration knotted her stomach. "It sure would help if I could figure out which of these numbers are important. And what they mean. I guess I have a bit more work to do."

"You can do it tomorrow. Evangeline has ordered me to take you home."

"Home?" He had to be joking. "Why so early?"

"It's not so early, Cassie. It's dinner time. Aren't you hungry?"

She glanced through the tech room's glass walls to the agent offices and cubicles. Lily's cropped blond head bowed over the copier, no doubt trying to fix it after Angel did another number on the darn thing. Cameron paced the terra-cotta tile near the conference room. And she could see veteran agent Ethan Moore through the glass walls of Evangeline's office, having one of his heart-to-hearts with the boss. No Angel. No Lenny. No John or Sara or any of the other agents who'd been in the office the last she'd looked. Could they have worked a full day and gone home or out for a dinner break while she'd been staring at the computer monitor?

She glanced back down at that monitor. Her shoulders sure hurt enough. But now that she'd had this breakthrough, she didn't want to quit.

"You do need food. And sleep," Mike said, as if reading where her thoughts were leading. "I talked to Evangeline. After what happened at your apartment this morning, we agreed it would be better if you stayed out at my ranch."

"What?" Had she misread his lips? Had he really just said that he and Evangeline had decided where she'd stay without consulting her? And at Mike's ranch, no less?

"Lily is going to stay at your apartment, in case our friends come back for another visit tonight. Cameron and Ethan are going to back her up."

"She's going to be a decoy?"

"Yes."

Why Lily? Why not her? Did they think she couldn't handle it? "Lily is shorter than me and she doesn't exactly have my hair color or style, either. No one's going to think she's me."

"She'll wear a wig and a pair of heels. It's not going to matter."

"But I could stay there just as easily as she can. No, more easily, since it's my home." She knew her voice was rising. She could feel the vibration in her throat. But she couldn't control it. Right now, she wanted to scream.

"Evangeline's orders. And I agreed with her."

"So that's it? The two of you have made your decision about what I would do, and you didn't even think to talk to me?"

"We both want you safe." He held up his

hand. "And don't go into some spiel about coddling the deaf girl. Keeping you alive isn't exactly coddling."

"Making decisions without talking to me is worse than coddling."

"Then you'll just have to hate me. Because I'm not going to let whoever the hell was at your apartment last night take another shot at you. And trying to make me feel guilty about it isn't going to work."

IT HAD TAKEN SOME DOING, but Mike had finally torn Cassie from her computer and forced her into her car, him at the wheel this time. They'd stopped at a fast-food restaurant and wolfed down hamburgers he was too tired to taste. Now he just had to get her back to the ranch where she could rest, with him and a state-of-the-art security system watching over her. In the battle over coddling the deaf girl, he'd won this round.

Not that he ever expected her to forgive him for it.

She sat in the passenger seat stiff as his dad's new saddle, her arms folded across her chest, her jacket pulled tight around her. Twilight had plunged the mountains outside the car into blue shadow. The dashboard light glowed green on Cassie's face, illuminating the hard clench of her jaw and turning her auburn hair nearly black.

Oh, well. He could handle her anger. Her contempt. As long as he didn't let her down when it came to what mattered—keeping her alive—he could handle anything.

The inside of the car was silent except for the light hum of pavement under the tires. Any other time he'd switch on the radio. But somehow listening to music didn't seem right. Not when Cassie couldn't share it with him.

He was about to steal one more glance in her direction when headlights flashed in the rearview mirror. Headlights from what looked like a BMW. Headlights on a road no cars had reason to be on.

He stiffened.

He could feel Cassie's gaze search his face in the dashboard glow. "What is it?"

He turned his head slightly so she could see his lips. "There's a car tailing us."

"How do you know? Couldn't he just be driving out this way?"

"Not unless he's lost. No one drives this highway this late at night, much less some guy in a BMW. And the only place out this way is mine. Besides, I saw this car earlier when we stopped for food."

"You think it's…" Her voice was hushed but calm. Calmer than he felt right now. "You think they're after me? After the disk?"

He'd bet on it. And after last night, he wouldn't be surprised if Mr. BMW was well armed.

Chapter Nine

Cassie gripped the armrest on the door with one hand and braced her other hand on the dash. Her heart pounded hard in her chest, making her teeth throb with each beat. The memory of watching that bullet explode off the brick wall slammed through her. And once again, she longed to cling to Mike, to wrap herself in the security of his arms and let him take care of her.

What was wrong with her?

She swallowed into a tight throat. Not willing to let Mike see how badly her hands were shaking, she forced her voice to function. "What are you going to do?"

He gripped the wheel, his hands calm, strong, in control. His lips moved, not a hint of the tremor she felt in her own. "I'm going to ask him why he's following us."

"What?" In her surprise, she realized she both spoke and signed the word.

"I'm going to ask him what the hell he thinks he's doing."

"How? By pulling over and rolling your window down?"

His lips curved into a smile. A confident, in-control, damn sexy smile.

What was she thinking? "You aren't really. Are you?"

"Watch."

She gripped the armrest harder and held on. She hadn't felt so out of control since college. But at the same time, she trusted Mike knew what he was doing, that it would work out.

And that strange sense of blind trust alone gave her reason to worry.

The engine of her little car started to whine. The dark, treeless swells outside her window whipped by. The road twisted this way, that way. Faster and faster. Leaving the BMW in the dust.

Cassie gripped the dash with one hand, the door with the other. She thought she might be sick.

"Hold on." Mike turned the wheel. Cassie's little car jetted to the left.

She gasped and held on. The car bumped and bucked under them, careening off the paved road and into a pair of dirt ruts she wasn't aware were there. They drove in a half circle.

Mike hit the brakes just before they returned to the road. Setting the emergency brake, he threw his door open. "Stay here."

In the flash of the dome light before the door closed, Cassie saw the gun in Mike's fist.

She clawed at the handle of her own door. Ripping it open, she half fell out into the dirt. She pushed the door closed, dousing the light.

She could see Mike's silhouette up ahead, dark against the moonlit road. She crept forward. She had no idea what she was doing out here. Or what she was going to do if anything bad happened. She might not be much when it came to backup, but she couldn't let Mike face whoever was following them alone.

She followed Mike's path. The road opened up before her. No, two roads. An intersection. Headlights emerged from around a curve and reflected off the stop sign.

Mike crouched between a jut of rock and

a patch of scrub brush. Cassie fitted herself in behind him.

He turned his face to the side, the moonlight giving a blue cast to hard features. "I thought I told you to stay in the car."

She raised her hands, choosing not to speak for fear she couldn't control the volume of her voice. *You need backup. And I'm it.*

"You're unarmed, Cassie. All you're going to be out here is a target."

I don't see that you have much choice in who backs you up here, Detective. Beggars can't be choosers.

Instead of a laugh, this time he shot her a warning look. "Stay here, then, will you? And if something goes wrong, hide."

On the road, the BMW approached the intersection. It slowed, then stopped. Cassie could almost feel the driver's confusion as he tried to decide which direction they'd taken.

Mike crept forward. Breaking into the exposure of the road, he launched into a run. He reached the BMW in a second, gun drawn and leveled on the car. His lips moved, body tense as if yelling.

Watching the scene from behind, Cassie wasn't sure what he was saying. But judging from the startled expression of the driver and the speed with which he shoved his hands into the air, Mike's ambush had worked the way he'd planned.

The driver spilled out of the car, his feet shuffling on the pavement as if he couldn't move fast enough. The BMW's dome light glowed from inside, exposing empty leather seats. The driver was alone.

Mike stood back from the man and barked orders Cassie couldn't make out, his gun still trained on the man.

Hands straight above his head, the man turned around slowly, until he had completed a 360-degree rotation. He laced his fingers on top of his head, lowered himself to his knees and crossed his ankles behind him.

Well-dressed in a leather jacket, designer label slacks and Italian loafers, the man sported a haircut and trimmed goatee that must have come from one of Denver's better salons. He sure looked like no thug Cassie had ever imagined. In the reflected light from his car, his face appeared to be flushed. Not as if he was afraid at all, but more as if he'd just finished his evening jog. He looked up at her, his eyelids slightly drooping.

Cassie found herself walking toward the car before she realized what she was doing. "Why are you following us?"

Mike held out a hand, warning her to stay back. He stepped to the man and ran his hand briskly over his sides. Then he backed up and moved to the side. "Okay, Cass. Come stand by me."

Cassie did as Mike directed.

"And you. Answer the question. Why are you following us?"

The man shook his head, his elbows swinging with the movement. "It's not what you think."

"How in the hell do you know what I think?" Mike gestured with the gun. "One more time."

The man's throat convulsed as if he was struggling to swallow. Or breathe. "I was afraid…I didn't know what else to do…I was afraid if I went to the offices, someone would see me."

"Offices?"

"Prescott Personal Securities' offices," he choked out.

Cassie forced her vocal chords to function. "Why are you trying to reach PPS?"

The man had the nerve to look at her as if she was no more important than a buzzing fly. Strange for a man who was on his knees with a gun barrel pointed at him.

He'd probably heard something off in the sound of her voice. Something that told him she wasn't normal as he saw it. Too bad she didn't care. "Answer."

He focused on Mike. "I need to hire you. I need protection."

"Why follow us? We're nearly an hour out of Denver."

"I went to the office, but I saw a car just sitting outside the building. I got nervous."

He didn't look nervous. He looked almost blasé. Cassie looked at Mike, hoping he was also picking up the strange vibe she was getting from this guy.

Mike's attention was on the man. "Why am I not inclined to believe you?"

"Listen. You don't know who I am." The man raised his chin, as if once they knew his identity they'd be falling all over themselves begging for his forgiveness.

"So who the hell are you?" Mike demanded.

"James Durgin."

The name didn't register with Cassie. Mike stared at him blankly as if waiting for the punch line.

"I'm CEO of Claypool Incorporated. You have heard of Claypool."

Cassie had. "It's an energy company, right?"

Durgin drew himself up with as much dignity as a man in his position could manage. "I'm an important man in Denver."

"Good for you," Mike said. "Now why should I care?"

"Because I'm next."

"Next?"

"Milo Kardascian called me the night before he died."

Mike stiffened.

Durgin drew himself up as if he'd finally found the power he'd sought. He peered down his nose at Mike's gun, quite a trick seeing that he was still on his knees. "Is the gun necessary?"

Mike didn't move. "What did Kardascian say?"

"Treat me with respect, or you don't need to know."

Mike canted the gun's barrel to the right side and down. But despite taking his aim off Durgin, Cassie could sense a tension in him ready to swing the gun back at any sudden movement. "Tell me about Kardascian. What did he say?"

"He said a lot of things." Now that Durgin was back in his familiar position of power, he'd apparently decided to milk it for all it was worth.

Cassie thought back to his comments about hiring PPS for protection. "I will speak with Evangeline about arranging protection for you as soon as possible. But not before you answer our questions."

Durgin gave her another one of those dismissive looks that made her blood boil. He focused on Mike. "Kardascian was scared. He said someone was out to kill him."

"Who?"

"He didn't know. But it had something to do with an investment we both recently made."

Mike glanced at Cassie and then back to Durgin. "What kind of investment?"

"I don't really know. It's a blind trust. You know, like the ones politicians are supposed to use to prevent conflicts of interest." He spoke carefully, slowly, as if they couldn't possibly understand. "I don't know what stocks they buy or who makes the decisions, but it is supposed to bring in a great profit. It all goes through an investment company."

Cassie didn't know much about investments, but the whole thing sounded pretty shady to her.

"So you don't know what you invested in or who controls it. Yet someone is trying to kill you?"

"That's what Kardascian said. And he said I'm next."

None of this added up, and Cassie got the impression he wasn't being as forthcoming as he wanted them to believe. She glanced at Mike.

He gave her a knowing nod. "Who else has invested in this blind trust?" Mike asked Durgin.

Durgin nodded slightly. He rubbed his lips

together before meeting her eyes. "I don't know. That's the blind part."

"Then how do you know Kardascian was an investor?"

"He called me."

"Out of the blue?"

"Kind of. I mean, I've met him before, but we never talked about the trust. He said he got a call that someone was trying to kill him and that I was next on the list. That's it. I thought it was a joke until yesterday."

Cassie suppressed the memory of Kardascian lying on the floor of his workout room, blood soaking his sweatshirt and the carpet beneath. No joke. "Do you know anyone else who has invested in this blind trust?" Cassie added.

He shifted his feet and glanced past Cassie, his gaze combing the surroundings.

"Answer," Mike said.

Durgin pulled at his goatee. "When we made the investment, each of us was given a contact name."

"A contact name for what?" Mike asked.

"I don't know."

Cassie frowned. She couldn't tell if he

didn't know or if he just didn't want to tell them. "And you were Kardascian's contact name?"

"That's what he said when he called."

Cassie glanced at Mike. If Kardascian had a contact name, Durgin must, too. "Who is your contact?"

He shook his head. "I never really had one."

"But you just said you were given a name when you made the investment."

"I was. I tried to contact him that day only to find out he'd been killed in a car accident years ago." He shook his head faster. "None of it made any sense."

Cassie had to agree there. Not that she was convinced Durgin really wanted to help them make sense out of anything. "So you're the end of the list, at least as far as we can trace it."

"Yeah." He glanced at the shadows around them, then focused on Mike. "I need protection. I need PPS. And if you don't mind, I really don't feel all that safe chatting out here in the middle of the road."

Cassie gnawed on the inside of her bottom lip. She didn't like it. Durgin's story didn't add up, and the way his eyes and flushed skin looked made her feel even more uncomfortable. He had to be hiding something. Or maybe she felt this way because he only talked to Mike and dismissed her. But whatever it was, she had a bad feeling about James Durgin.

She glanced at Mike. *I don't trust him.*

Mike nodded. *Me, either. But he might have answers. Answers we need.*

Durgin looked at them through eyelids at half mast. "What are you saying?"

Cassie focused back on Mike. *There's something not right about him.*

Mike's chest shook in a laugh. *There's a lot that's not right about him. But I assume you're talking about the drugs.*

Drugs?

Heroin is my guess.

She'd never considered he was a druggie, but it made sense. There was a whole lot Mr. I'm An Important Man wasn't telling them. A prickle of unease rose up Cassie's spine and centered at her nape. And they had to get to the bottom of it. "I'll get my car. You can crouch down on the floor while Mike keeps his gun handy. It might not be your idea of the 'respect you deserve,' but it's the only way you're getting to PPS without being spotted."

MIKE STEPPED into the PPS office where Evangeline had ushered Durgin when they arrived. His body felt charged with an intoxicating rush of adrenaline. Interviewing subjects had always been his favorite part of police work. And with a self-important junkie scumbag like Durgin, cutting to the truth would be even more fun. Since the mess with the Dirty Three had begun, he'd almost forgotten how much he loved being on the job. Or at least as close as he could get at the moment. His blood was buzzing with it.

He let his gaze skim over the rich gold walls and spare, Western-inspired furnishings. Evangeline promised there would be a camera in this office to record the interview, but he sure couldn't see one.

From a chair positioned at the side of the large oak desk, James Durgin looked up at him with half-hooded eyes. If Mike hadn't had experience dealing with people under the influence of drugs, he might not have recognized Durgin's impairment. But the signs were there.

This would be a piece of cake.

Mike pulled out the desk chair and folded himself into it, his knees separated from Durgin's by the corner of the desk.

"You filled out the paperwork?"

"Enough of it." Durgin darted his eyes away, his pupils looking more constricted than Mike had noticed out on the dark mountain road. He tossed the form on the desk.

Mike glanced at it. Durgin had printed his name, address and all the other relevant information in a precise if slightly shaking hand. There was only one section left blank. "You didn't fill out your financial information."

"Trust me. I have the money to cover PPS's fees."

"Where? In that blind trust of yours?"

"Some of it. Also in various other accounts and assets. Money is not a problem for a man like me."

Right. Mike almost smiled. Whenever someone like Durgin answered questions in such an absolute way yet refused to give details, Mike could bet he was lying. "You and Kardascian. Claypool and Vasco Pharmaeceuticals. Wealthy pillars of the community. I forgot."

Durgin snickered.

"Care to share what's so amusing?"

"You didn't know?"

"Know what?"

"Kardascian doesn't own controlling shares in Vasco Pharm anymore."

This was easier than Mike dreamed. "He sold his stock in his company? Why? Was Vasco in some sort of financial crisis?"

"Not that I know of. But Kardascian is... was."

Mike shook his head. "I've been to his so-called cabin. He didn't look like he was hurting too badly."

"In debt to the top of his balding dome."

"I don't believe you."

Durgin drew back, as if offended. "He's been spending most of his time in the best private gambling clubs all around Denver. And some of the limited-stakes ones, too. I know a girl, a blackjack dealer."

Gambling. Interesting. "So is gambling

something you and Kardascian also have in common?"

Durgin glared as if it was blasphemy to suggest such a thing. "No."

"So how does someone like you get to know a blackjack dealer?"

"I met her at a society party. One of those casino night shindigs that raise money for charity. That's all." He stroked his goatee, a self-grooming tick that almost always accompanied a lie. "That's the only time I've seen her."

"You sure about that?"

"Maybe I saw her a different time. Another charity event. I don't keep track of staff at parties."

"Let me guess. You needed something to take the edge off giving money to the needy, and she said she could get her hands on a little smack."

Durgin shifted in his chair. "I don't know what you're talking about."

"And she not only came through, she knew where she could get more. As much as you wanted."

"I don't do drugs."

"Really?" Mike reached out and caught the CEO's hand. He flattened the man's palm to the desk and spread his fingers. Needle tracks packed the webs between the digits. "What are those, Jimmy? Bug bites?"

"So I tried it. That doesn't mean I use."

"No, it probably means you've already used the veins between your toes so you've had to resort to your hands. And it looks like it won't be long until you're going to run out of hidden places to stick your needle."

"Okay. I'm trying to kick the stuff. I'm checking into rehab next week. You can verify that."

Mike didn't really care about Durgin's plans for rehabilitation. In his experience, junkies always intended to check into rehab next week. Problem was, next week never became now. He was more interested in the things Durgin had in common with Kardascian. "What's the name of this blackjack dealer and where can I find her?"

Durgin stared at Mike with his pinprick pupils. "I…I don't remember."

Mike pulled his cell phone from his belt. He didn't have time for this garbage. "Well, then, you might want to cancel those reservations at your cushy rehab center. I'm sure my partner, Detective Tim Grady, wouldn't mind making some arrangements for you at the county jail. I hear cold turkey is the way to go anyway."

"Lila."

"Last name?"

"Starts with an *S*."

"Where can I find her?"

"She works up in Central City now. She deals at one of those Old West casinos. Until the last few weeks, she worked in a private club for high rollers. Said Milo lost more in that club than most people make in their lifetime." He sat up, his lids opening fully, as if he'd suddenly found the answer. "Her last name is Strotsky, or something like that."

Russian? Mike's gut clenched. In Denver, a Russian name mixed with gambling and drugs added up to bad news. "Some of those private gambling clubs have ties to the Russian Mafiya. Did you know that?"

Durgin glanced around the room as if looking for a way out. Apparently not finding one, he slumped in his chair. "No. I wasn't aware. I don't know anything about that stuff."

"They are big players in the drug trade, too. Especially heroin from Afghanistan."

Durgin paled.

Mike didn't blame him. If the Russian mob was part of this mess, Durgin was facing serious danger...and until that disk was decrypted, so was Cassie.

Chapter Ten

Mike stepped from the office turned interview room and into the adjoining suite. Gathered around an oversized flat screen monitor sat Cassie, Evangeline, the black-taloned receptionist who'd ushered him into the offices yesterday, and an agent he recognized from the news coverage of movie star Nick Warner's ill-fated visit to Denver. Jack Sanders, if memory served.

Evangeline greeted him with a smile. "Now that was an interrogation. Remind me never to lie to you, Detective Lawson." She glanced over her shoulder. "Angel?"

The receptionist stopped chewing her gum. She whipped her head around to face Evangeline, her spiked black hair sharp enough to cut someone. "Yeah?"

"Would you please escort Mr. Durgin to

the office living quarters and fix him up with clean linens and toiletries?"

Apparently Evangeline trusted Durgin a hell of a lot more than Mike did. "You're letting him stay here?"

"For tonight. That way we can keep an eye on him."

Angel shuffled past Mike. Her black lip-sticked lips curved into a shy yet flirty smile as she passed him and let herself into the office where Durgin waited. After the door closed, her image appeared on the monitor, talking to Durgin, metal flashing from her pierced tongue each time she opened her mouth.

Mike pulled his eyes from the strange sight and moved into the room to take the seat next to Cassie.

Before they could start, the red-haired tech guy Mike had also met yesterday popped his head in from the outer office. "The new cameras work?"

"Beautifully, Lenny." Evangeline gave him a warm smile. "I don't know what we'd do without you."

Lenny blushed a little, mumbled something and wandered away, as if his mind had already jumped to the next technological challenge on his agenda.

Evangeline cleared her throat and turned to the three of them remaining in the room. She looked past Mike and Cassie and focused on Sanders. "Jack? Thanks for postponing your trip to L.A. I know I promised to give you some time off with Kelly and Alexandra."

"They understand. Well, Kelly does. Alexandra is a different story. You know four-year-olds."

Evangeline gave Jack a warm smile. "We won't keep you from them too long. I hope."

"Whatever it takes."

"Glad to hear it. I need you to see what you can find out about Kardascian's finances and the sale of his business. And see what you can find out about Durgin, too."

Jack nodded and turned to Mike and Cassie. "So let me make sure I have all this straight. Milo Kardascian had money problems due to a gambling habit, so he sold his business to Tri Corp Media, right?"

Mike nodded. "I'm assuming the sale to TCM gave him the money to invest in this blind trust, but you might want to check that."

"And Durgin?"

"I wouldn't be surprised if you find he also had a debt problem. Heroin can get expensive. And who knows what else that guy is into."

"So what is with this blind trust?" Cassie asked. "Why would Kardascian and Durgin sink their money into something they didn't have control over and didn't know who did?"

"Several possibilities. Money laundering for one."

Cassie's eyes widened. "For the Russian mob?"

"If they were in deep from their gambling and drug habits, the mob might have used the debt to leverage a little assistance cleaning dirty money."

"And if the mob isn't involved?"

The option Mike was hoping for. "If the mob isn't involved, a blind trust would still give them plausible deniability."

Cassie arched her eyebrows in question.

"If the trust dabbles in investments that cross the line of the law, Kardascian and Durgin can say they didn't know anything about it."

"And get away with it."

Mike nodded. "The rich operate under different laws than the rest of us."

Jack's jaw hardened. He looked back to Evangeline. "Do you want me to check out this Lila Strotsky, too?"

"No. You have enough to follow up on. I'll have Sara do it. She's on the surveillance team at Cassie's apartment right now, but she can get on it first thing tomorrow."

Mike shifted in his chair. If he remembered correctly who Sara was, she'd struck him as being a bit young for the job. "Why Sara?"

Evangeline smiled, as if she found the question amusing. "Sara might look like she's about sixteen years old, but she's not. She's former FBI. She has contacts in the Organized Crime Division that will give her a lot more information than we can get on our own."

"I see." Sara's contacts probably could shed some much needed light, but he still didn't like waiting. He wanted to know exactly what kind of danger Cassie was facing. He resisted the urge to glance in Cassie's direction. With her ability to read him, she'd probably recognize the protectiveness he felt right off... and get mad at him for coddling her all over again.

"Jack?" Evangeline said, bringing the conversation back to the track she'd been on when

Mike interrupted. "If you need help, see if John Pinto can spare a moment. He and Ethan are setting up the security cameras for Congressman Tracker's fund-raiser tomorrow."

"Will do." Jack thrust himself up from his chair. He stood so straight, Mike half expected him to salute. Had to be ex-military.

"What about Mike and me?" Cassie said.

A wave of concern passed over Evangeline's face. She took a breath, quickly hiding the emotion, but Mike was sure Cassie had seen it. He could feel her tense beside him.

"We can't just sit around and do nothing," Cassie prodded.

"That's exactly what you need to do. Go to Mike's ranch. Rest. I need your mind to be fresh."

"I don't need rest. I need to work on the disk. I need to find answers."

"You said you'd deciphered the disk, that you just don't know what the numbers mean."

Cassie nodded. "That's why I should be here, working on it."

"No. That's why you need some rest. Tomorrow you might be able to see it in a whole new light. Besides, our minds solve some of our toughest problems while we're sleeping."

Mike didn't think Cassie bought Evangeline's theory. But then, he'd learned that Cassie didn't believe anything just happened. Not without her making it happen. It was part of what he found so refreshing about her, if frustrating at times.

"All right then, we're done." Evangeline stood. She and Jack filed out of the room quickly, leaving Cassie and Mike alone. Cassie pursed her lips together and skewed them to the side.

An uneasy feeling pinched Mike's gut. "You're planning something, aren't you?"

Cassie gave him an innocent look. *What time is it?*

In the past day, she'd largely given up signing. The fact that she was returning to it now made Mike all the more uneasy. He checked his watch. *Eleven o'clock,* he signed back.

Then there's still time.

He braced himself, waiting for the other shoe to fall. *Time for what?*

Blackjack.

Suddenly her signing made sense. She didn't want Evangeline or one of the others in the office to overhear her plan. He should have known. He thought about how she ran out onto the road when he'd stopped Durgin, no thought for her own safety. He could see why her family would worry about her, but it didn't have anything to do with her deafness. The woman needed a keeper.

Good thing that was his assignment.

He shook his head. *We're going to the ranch. I want you where I know you'll be safe.*

I don't need to huddle at your ranch the whole night in order to be safe. I need to find out what is going on. She shot him a determined glare. *I'm going to find Lila Strotsky, no matter what you and Evangeline say. Now you can be my backup or get out of the way.*

Mike let out a breath. He had the feeling it was going to be a long night.

MIKE AND CASSIE STRODE down Eureka Street toward Main. He could feel the weight of the pistol holstered on his belt with each step. He surveyed the flat, gingerbread facades of the restored gold-mining town, waiting…

For what? A Russian mobster to spring out from one of the casinos or gift shops like an Old West gunfighter and gun them down in the streets?

He forced a breath of thin mountain air. He couldn't let his worry for Cassie's safety make him paranoid. He had to get focused. He touched Cassie's arm. "So what are you planning to learn from Lila Strotsky that you don't think Sara can get from the FBI?"

"I want to know if she works with the Russian mob and if they are the ones behind this blind trust."

"Oh, that's all. Nothing like being ambitious. You don't think she's just going to tell you, do you?"

"No. But I saw how you handled Durgin. I figure she'll tell you." She looked at him out of the corner of her eye and grinned.

"Thanks for the vote of confidence. But if Lila is involved with the mob, she's not going to be that easy to handle."

"Then threaten her."

"With what?"

"Jail. For selling drugs to Durgin. Tell her you'll call the police, just like you did with Durgin."

"I don't think she'll be scared, Cassie. The Russian mob has a habit of buying police." He stopped in his tracks. His heart throbbed loud in his ears. Why in the hell hadn't he made that connection before?

"What is it?"

"The Dirty Three. You know, the narcotics detectives I turned in to Internal Affairs."

"You think they might be tied to the Russian mob?"

"I don't know. Maybe. I lost my gun the night they used me for a punching bag, then it turned up in Kardascian's murder. I don't think anyone in their right mind could believe in a coincidence like that."

"So the Dirty Three work for whoever is controlling this blind trust?"

"Maybe. Or maybe they're on that list of investors. Hard to tell." Suddenly he wanted very much to talk to Lila Strotsky. Even if Sara Montgomery's contacts could give them more information than he and Cassie could likely get tonight, he needed to find out whatever he could right away.

He needed to know who to trust.

They continued walking to the intersection

of Main and Eureka Streets and turned into the historic Teller House. Finding their way into the casino, they located the blackjack tables.

"Care to play?" A dark-skinned dealer with a wide, pink lipsticked smile motioned them over to her table.

Mike stepped up to the padded rail. The air was alive with the chime of electronic bells and blips of slot machines. He leaned close and asked, "Is Lila working?"

"I think so." The smiling dealer glanced around the tables. "Oh, I guess she's not."

"Do you know where we can find her? We really need to talk to her. I'm Detective Lawson of the Denver PD and this is Agent Allen." He could feel Cassie smile at the title he'd given her.

The dealer's smile turned wary. "She's not in any trouble, is she?"

"No. It's just routine. We think she might have witnessed a car accident."

The dealer nodded, her smile returning with toothpaste-commercial brilliance. "Ask at the bar. Sophie, the bartender, is a friend of Lila's."

"Thanks."

Inside The Face Bar, Cassie stopped at a small wood railing protecting a square of plank floor. "It's the painting. *The Face On The Barroom Floor.* The one they say a cowboy painted while pining for his lost love."

Mike followed her gaze. Sure enough, the famous face area legends had been spun over stared up at him. A woman with the same heart-shaped face, sparkling eyes and curly auburn hair as Cassie.

His throat suddenly pinched. He didn't know how the cowboy in the legend had lost this woman he loved, but he didn't really want to find out. He didn't want to think about it at all. Hell, he'd heard that legend wasn't even true.

He brushed Cassie's arm with his fingertips. "There's the bartender."

She tore her focus from the portrait and followed him to the bar.

"Welcome to The Face Bar. What can I get you?" The bartender's smile was almost as blinding as the blackjack dealer's.

"We're looking for Lila."

"You're interested in a puppy?"

A puppy? Mike nodded. Might as well play along. "Very interested. Lila said she'd be working tonight. We were going to talk puppies."

"She was scheduled to work. But she called off at the last minute." The woman looked from him to Cassie. "So you two are looking to adopt one of those cute little dogs, huh? They're so adorable."

"I can't wait to see them." Cassie nodded, playing right along. "Do you have any idea how we can get in touch with her?"

"She had some flyers around here." The bartender's blond head ducked behind the bar. When she came up, she had a flyer in her hand.

Mike took the piece of paper. A fluffy little poodlelike dog stared out at him. Not exactly a ranch dog. He looked down the page. Printed on the bottom was Lila's name and a phone number.

"She stays up late," the bartender was saying. "You can probably still call her now."

Mike nodded. "Thanks." But calling wasn't

what he had in mind. He would have Grady plug it into the reverse directory and give him the address.

TRADER GULCH ROAD was a long stretch that twisted through the mountains. Beautiful country in the daytime. A precarious, dark maze at night. As Mike wound around hairpin turns and looked over cliffs falling to black, all he could think about was how much he wished he had his truck.

"It shouldn't be much farther," Cassie said. She pointed to a house number at the base of a driveway that led to a house on the top of the ridge.

"Anytime would be nice," he said between gritted teeth as he followed the road around another impossible turn.

"Look." Cassie pointed up the road.

Red and blue lights pulsed through the darkness, making the branches of budding aspen stand in stark relief, like black skeletons.

Mike took his foot off the gas, letting the car slow to a crawl. They rounded the curve ahead.

Two Gilpin County Sheriff's cars clustered

around a driveway, light bars flashing. The driveway snaked up to a mansion clinging to the side of the rising mountain. A deputy stood by the cars, stretching a ribbon of yellow crime-scene tape across the driveway's mouth and tying it off around a mailbox marked with the name Strotsky.

Chapter Eleven

Cassie's heart pulsed in time with the flashing police lights. Pressure bore down on her chest, making it hard to breathe. "My God. Do you think she's dead?"

Mike's face looked pale in the light from the dash and the pulsing red and blue. "We aren't going to wait around to find out. The last thing I want to do is try to explain why we're showing up at another crime scene." He shifted the car into Reverse, backing around the bend until he found a spot on the shoulder to turn around.

"Where are we going?"

"To the ranch. Where I know you'll be safe."

Safe. What had sounded like hovering just a few hours ago sounded good now. Probably too good. She shook her head, banishing the image of breaking down in the doorway last night. Taking in a deep breath, she gripped her thighs with shaking hands. She was going to remain strong this time, prove what she was made of, that she didn't need hovering and coddling and special favors to deal with anything life threw at her.

Even murder.

She focused on the questions buzzing in her mind. "Do you think it could be the Russian mob? Do you think they hurt her? Or worse?"

"She sure isn't able to afford that house on what she makes as a blackjack dealer. And we know she got heroin from somewhere."

"So what do we do?"

"Hold on." Mike pulled off on a side road and took his cell phone from his belt. He flipped it open, punched in a number and held the phone to his ear. After a few beats, he nodded. "Grady. Remember that address you found for me? Looks like something's going on that I need you to look into."

Mike related what they'd found and Lila Strotsky's name and address to his partner. "Thanks, buddy. I owe you. Yeah, yeah, yeah. Again." He folded the phone.

"He's going to call back?"

"He's going to find out what he can." Mike pulled the car back on the road leading to his ranch. "He said there was a report of a homicide in Gilpin County."

"That has to be it, doesn't it. With that many sheriff's cars, what else could it be?"

"We'll wait and see."

They didn't have to wait too long. Barely fifteen minutes had passed when Mike pulled off and reached for his phone. "Lawson."

Cassie watched his expression, his face unchanging in the green glow of the dash. He murmured a few words into the phone, meaningless yeses and "I see."

Cassie dug her fingertips into her thighs. There were countless times over the years that she wished she could still hear. But none were more sharp and urgent than right now.

Finally he stowed the phone and turned to face her. "She's dead. Killed sometime tonight. They can't be sure when."

Cassie leaned back in her seat. The tremble that had started when she saw the police lights swept over her in force. Another murder. "How did they know we were looking for her? The casino?"

Mike shook his head. "Not if the sheriff was already at the scene. Not enough time."

"Maybe she was on the list of investors in that blind trust."

Mike shook his head. "Durgin was supposed to be next, if he can be believed. I suspect she could provide the link between Kardascian and Durgin and whoever it is that's behind this blind trust."

"And they killed her before we could talk to her?"

"Maybe."

"How did they know we found out about her? The only people who knew work for PPS."

Mike's lips didn't move.

She shook her head. "It couldn't be someone at PPS."

"I'm not saying it is. Lila was tied to Kardascian and Durgin. That could be reason right there for someone to kill her."

Cassie nodded. "Yes. I'm sure that's it."

"Whoever killed her, it's probably safe to assume she knew something someone wanted to keep quiet."

Cassie thought about the mess in her apartment last night. The bullet hitting the brick wall inches from her head. The car rolling quietly past the pedestrian mall, searching for her hiding place. "They wanted to silence Lila. Just like they want to silence me."

Mike released the wheel and patted her forearm.

She knew the gesture was meant to be reassuring, but that familiar longing to curl up in his arms and forget all of this was anything but.

He withdrew his hand and turned his attention back to the road ahead, leaving a void where his warmth had been.

Silence hung heavy in the car the rest of the drive to Mike's ranch. Finally they reached the intersection where they'd confronted Durgin. His BMW was gone, picked up by one of the PPS agents. The whole event felt as if it was so long ago, even though it had been only been a few hours. So much had changed, yet they weren't any closer to discovering who was behind these murders or the disk or the attempt on her life. The only thing that was really different was now the ominous shadow of the Russian mob loomed on the horizon.

"This is it." Mike swung the truck onto a gravel road.

Ponderosa pine, cottonwood and aspen fell away and a valley opened in front of them. With only light from the stars, she couldn't make out much of the small ranch, but she did spot what looked like two houses, one with soft light burning in the windows, a couple of structures that looked like barns and what seemed like miles of wood fence. All sides of the valley climbed upward, some sides heavily wooded, some slopes bare grass and rock. "I bet it's beautiful in the daytime."

"It is. It's a long commute, but I love it here."

"How could you afford it? Land like this, in the mountains, it can't be cheap."

"I inherited it. From my mother's side of the family."

It felt good to be talking about normal things. Family. Land. Not mobsters and murder. "How do you run a ranch and work as a police detective?"

"I don't. Not really."

She gave him a funny look, half confusion, half suspicion he was nuts.

He chuckled. She might not have been able to hear the sound, but she could feel it in the air around her. She could see it in the slight smoothing of the stress lines around his mouth, illuminated by the dashboard's soft green light.

She liked the feeling his laugh gave her, as if she was giving something back to him. A gift he deeply needed.

His lips formed an explanation. "First, it's not a working ranch. It's more of a hobby ranch. We don't have cattle, just a few horses."

"But even just a few horses take a lot of work."

"True. We didn't have any animals until my dad retired from the force. That's when he moved out here and got into horses. He has six quarter horses now. He was supposed to be breeding and selling them, but he's more into breeding and keeping them. He lives over there." He pointed to the house with the light in its window, then swung the truck toward the darkened house. "This is my place."

The house looked like a ranch house from an old Western with gray clapboard siding and a porch that encircled three sides of the home. It even had a rocking chair perched near the front door.

Cassie smiled, soaking in the normalcy of it all like a soothing balm. "It's charming."

"It was my grandparents' house when I was growing up. I couldn't bring myself to change anything about it. Well, not much, anyway. I did add a dishwasher."

"Smart man."

He stopped the car next to the porch steps and they both climbed out into the cool night.

Cassie drew in a deep breath. There was nothing more fragrant and clean than spring in the mountains. She could see why Mike would deal with the long drive to Denver. Living in a beautiful spot like this was more than worth it.

Mike pulled the overnight bag Lily had packed for Cassie out of the trunk, led her up the stairs and unlocked the door. Before ushering her inside, he entered a security code into the touch pad inside to turn off the alarm. "All clear." He motioned her into the house.

She stepped past him, catching his scent as she brushed by. He smelled as crisp and clean as the air outside. Yet earthy, too. Sensual. The memory of his arms around her, his lips on hers kicked up that tremor in her chest. Suddenly she was hyperaware of how alone they were. Just the two of them. With nothing but the night around them.

She gave her head a shake. She couldn't let herself fantasize. That would only lead her places she didn't want to go. She'd spent too long building her life. Too long learning to be strong. Too long to fall back into the weakness of relying on someone else to take care of her.

If she ever had a relationship with a man again, she wasn't going to enter it out of weakness. She wasn't going to fall for a guy just to feel safe. She wanted a partner, not a protector. And as much as she was starting to feel for Mike, he had protector written all over him. Not just as a result of his role as her bodyguard, but as the most prominent part of his personality. *Evangeline ordered me to get some rest, so I'd better get to it.*

She wasn't sure why she'd returned to signing. Somehow speaking seemed too intimate. And without knowing how her voice sounded, too out of her control.

Mike exhaled as if relieved as she was to have the moment broken. He led her through a comfortable if overly manly living room furnished with a gun cabinet, several Western-looking leather chairs and a couch upholstered with a nubby red fabric that looked like burlap.

Turning, he climbed the wood-railed staircase next to the mouth of the darkened kitchen and motioned to a door at the end of the hall. "That's the guest bedroom. And next to it is the bath."

"Thanks," she said abruptly. "Good night." She ripped her gaze from him and forced her feet to move down the hall, feeling his gaze on her—and the need to return it—all the way.

CASSIE OPENED the door of the guest bedroom, half-hoping to see Mike out in the hall. The hall was vacant, a light still glowing downstairs from what she guessed was the kitchen.

Breathing a sigh of relief, she made her way toward the bathroom. She'd slipped on the sweatpants and sweatshirt Lily had packed for her, no doubt making herself look like a dark gray blob. Just as well. The last thing she wanted was to look sexy if Mike happened to run into her on her short trip to the bathroom.

Reaching the little room, she paused outside. Something didn't seem right.

Was she imagining things?

No. It was there. Something different.

Something strange about the feel of the place that hadn't existed when she and Mike had arrived. If she could hear, she might have been able to detect what had changed. But with the permanent silence in her head, she could only rely on feeling. Scents. The pressure in the air. The energy she felt through some sort of sixth sense.

Negative energy.

The back of her neck prickled. She glanced back at the door to her room. If something bad was happening in the house, hiding wasn't going to save her. Especially since it was her they were after.

Besides, there was no way she was going to leave Mike to face it alone.

She forced herself to breathe. She had to keep her head together. She had to remain calm. When they'd entered the house, she'd noticed a gun cabinet in the living room. Hunting rifles. She only prayed there was ammunition to go with them.

She stepped down the stairs, trying to make as little sound as possible. Not that she would know it if she failed, but anyone else in the house certainly would. Light streamed from the kitchen and fell across the hardwood floor. She skirted the edge of the light and stepped into the living room's shadow.

The gun cabinet stood at the far side of the room. The glass doors reflected the light, making it hard to see inside. But she thought she caught the outlines of three, maybe four, long guns. All she needed was one. She scampered across the wood floor. At least she was wearing socks. That should muffle any sound her light footsteps made.

Reaching the cabinet, she grabbed the handle and pulled. The door didn't budge. Locked? She bent down, trying to see in the dim light. The key. She needed to find the cabinet's key.

She fitted her hand between cabinet and wall, groping for a hook, a nail, any place where Mike might stash a key. Nothing. She stepped to the adjacent bookshelf and repeated the process. Again, she came up empty.

Where would Mike hide the cabinet's key?

If she broke the glass, the sound would give her away. But if she wasted any more time…

The alarm prickling the back of her neck had long since turned to sheer, blaring panic. Something was wrong in the house. She could sense it throbbing in the air. Screaming along her nerves like an alarm.

She focused on a small rolltop desk tucked into the cove under the stairs. Opening the top, she groped through the papers, address book and checkbook lying on top of a laptop computer. She felt her way through cubbyholes filled with bills and receipts. Her fingers touched something cool and metallic. She grasped the key and returned to the gun cabinet.

Her hands trembled, so badly she could barely fit the key into the lock. It turned under her fingers. Opening the door, she grabbed one of the rifles.

Ammunition. She needed to find the bullets and see if she remembered how to load a rifle. She yanked open the drawers underneath the gun rack. Cleaning supplies. No ammunition. Where in the world would Mike keep the ammunition?

A strong vibration shook the air. Even though she couldn't hear the sound, she could feel it. Loud. Sudden. Something was happening. Something was going down right now.

She gripped the gun and made for the

kitchen. She'd have to bluff. If pressed, she couldn't do much with an unloaded rifle, but that didn't matter. She had no idea where the ammunition could be. And she couldn't risk that something was happening right now, that Mike would be hurt, that if she didn't get in there she would be too late.

She crept quickly across the wood floor, holding the rifle in front of her as she'd learned hunting with her dad and brother when she was a teenager. Her socks skidded on the floor. She struggled, regaining her balance and darted around the corner and into the kitchen.

The bright light blinded her for a second. She squinted, willing her eyes to adjust. A man was in the kitchen with Mike, his back to her. Silver hair, broad shoulders. He spun around.

He looked so familiar that at first she thought she must be seeing things. Almost black eyes peered out from a thin, weathered face. He had the same nose, the same chin, in everything but age and bruises, he looked like Mike would in twenty or so years.

Cassie looked past the man and met

Mike's surprised eyes. He stared at the rifle in her hands. "Cassie? This is my dad. Dad? This is Cassie."

EMBARRASSMENT CREPT up Cassie's neck and suffused her pale cheeks with color. She lowered the rifle, pointing the barrel at the floor. "Mr. Lawson…I'm sorry…I thought something happened. I thought something was wrong."

His dad nodded, his body on alert, his hand hovering near the Glock he, like many retired cops, kept at his side.

Guilt dug into Mike's chest. He knew what had frightened Cassie. She might not have been able to hear him and his dad yelling at each other, but that didn't mean she couldn't feel it. More than once, Tommy had reacted to angry or alarmed voices, and he had never known what hearing was.

Mike stepped past his dad, and she handed him the rifle. "I'm sorry, Cass. It was just us. We were arguing." He bit back the urge to add *picking up where we left off*.

His dad scrutinized Cassie with the same narrowed gaze Mike had suffered under through countless interrogations as a teenager.

And since. A gaze that saw everything. He raised his hands. *I'm sorry we alarmed you. Sometimes I get carried away. We both do.*

Leave it to his dad to realize Cassie was deaf. But then, he remembered Tommy, too.

He turned his scrutiny on Mike, as if trying to figure out what was going on between him and Cassie without asking.

Mike wasn't about to attempt to explain. His dad would only read things into their relationship that weren't there. And no doubt, he'd end up disappointed in Mike for some reason or other. No, the shorter Mike could make this visit, the better. "Cassie has a busy day tomorrow, Dad. If you don't mind—"

"You want me to leave."

Mike pressed his lips together in an unspoken yes.

"Maybe that's for the best." He turned to Cassie, giving her a stiff, coplike nod. *Nice meeting you, Cassie. Again, I'm sorry for alarming you.*

Please, don't apologize. Cassie offered a shaky smile. *I'm sorry for pointing a gun at you.*

His dad chuckled, the sound warmer than

anything Mike had heard from his lips in twenty years. *I guess we're even then.*

Cassie smiled. *I guess we are.*

His dad let himself out the kitchen door. As soon as it shut behind him, Cassie's smile dissolved into a look of concern. "What was going on?"

"What do you mean?"

"What do I mean? The tension between your dad and you was thick enough to choke on."

He let out a breath. He didn't want to talk about this. Not with Cassie. Not with anyone. And definitely not now. "It's nothing. My dad and I just don't get along too well."

She gave him a sideways look.

He should leave it at that, not say anything more. But somehow, the way she looked at him made him feel compelled to fill the silence with words. Like all the suspects he'd ever interrogated. "I've disappointed him. That's all."

"Disappointed him? How?"

It would be easier to list the ways he hadn't disappointed his father. He grabbed at the most straightforward. "He's a cop. Born and bred."

"He's upset about your suspension?"

"Not just the suspension. All of it. I lost my gun. I'm a suspect in a homicide. I ratted out my fellow cops."

"How can he be upset that you turned in officers who were stealing? Isn't upholding the law your job?"

"It's not quite that easy. Not with cops. We have to rely on one another to get through each day alive. We can't afford to turn on each other. Not for any reason."

"That's what your dad thinks?"

"Like I said, he's a cop. Deputy chief by the time he retired."

She nodded, her eyebrows dipping low. "I guess I just can't believe your dad feels that way, too."

Mike let out a breath. As upset as he was with his dad, he didn't want Cassie blaming him for something that was out of his control. "My dad's right. Even the most law-abiding citizen will turn on police the moment he gets a traffic ticket, deserved or not. If cops can't rely on cops, who can they rely on?"

"Trusting one another and allowing each other to break the law are two different things."

"That's true in theory, but people's feelings aren't always logical." His feelings sure weren't logical. Especially lately. Especially around Cassie.

"So why did you do it? Why did you turn in those officers?"

There was only one answer to that question. "Because it was the right thing to do."

"But you're paying such a price for it."

"I promised. I promised I'd do the right thing. No matter what it cost me."

"Promised who?"

He shouldn't have said anything. He didn't want to talk about this. "No one. Myself, I guess. I don't know."

"Promised who, Mike? You can talk to me."

"I know I can." Hell, she'd probably try to reassure him. Tell him he was young. Tell him his impatience was understandable. Maybe even tell him his parents had expected too much of him. He knew all the lines, all the rationalizations. He'd tried every single one on for size. But when it got down to it, Tommy was still gone. And it was still his fault. And no explanations or sympathy or understanding would change what he'd done.

Pressure built behind his eyes. "It's late. We both need some shut—"

The pop of gunfire sounded from outside.

Adrenaline slammed through him. "Get down!"

Cassie stared at him, confused and unmoving.

Chapter Twelve

Mike grabbed Cassie's arm and pulled her to the floor. His heart raced, beating against his ribs with bruising force.

Dad. Dad was outside.

He grabbed the rifle Cassie had brought into the kitchen. Staying as low as he could, he reached for Nana's ancient sugar canister and grabbed a handful of rifle cartridges. He loaded the rifle and stuffed a handful in his pocket.

"Stay here. And stay low. Understand?"

Cassie nodded. She looked pale but determined. The way she'd looked when she'd burst into the kitchen, rifle at the ready.

He could only pray the shots outside were a similar false alarm. His dad firing to scare off a cougar prowling near the barn. A bear trying to get into their trash despite the fencing surrounding it. Something. Anything. Flicking off the kitchen light, he opened the door and slipped out onto the porch.

He crept across the porch, remaining low. He didn't see his dad out on the road between the houses. He didn't see anything.

Making it down the steps, he stuck close to the bushes near the side of the house. What he wouldn't give for some solid rock for cover instead of these pitiful-looking bushes, just starting to leaf out for summer. He peered through the darkness, his eyes starting to adjust to the moonlight's blue glow. No sounds came from the barn. Nothing moved.

The shuffle of footsteps on wood came from behind him.

He spun around, leading with the rifle barrel.

A shadow crouched on the porch. Moonlight glowed dull on a rifle barrel and gleamed dark red on shoulder-length curls.

Cassie.

He pulled the barrel down and lowered the rifle. He wanted to order her back in the house. He wanted her as far from this unknown danger as she could get. But he knew she'd never listen.

Hell, she'd probably inform him that she was his backup.

Holding up a hand, he motioned her toward him, reminding her to stay low.

She scampered off the porch and burrowed into the bushes beside him.

I thought I told you to stay inside, he signed, glad to have a silent way to communicate.

And do what? Wait for them to come in and get me? It's not like I can hear them approach.

She had a point. He nodded to her weapon. *Do you know how to use that thing?*

My dad and brother hunt. I haven't shot a rifle for years, but I used to be pretty good.

Okay. Stick close. At least he'd know where she was. And whoever was out there wouldn't.

A shadow moved near the barn.

Mike narrowed his eyes, struggling to see through the darkness. Was it a man? An animal?

A flash of light. The crack of gunfire.

Mike flattened himself to the ground, pulling Cassie with him. Damn. It was a man, all right. A man who was shooting at them. "This is Detective Lawson of the Denver PD. Put down your weapon. Now."

Another round fired from the shadows of the barn. The report echoed off the house behind their backs, then reverberated again off the rocky ridge surrounding the valley.

Breath roaring in his ears, Mike raised his head just enough to look around. Where was his dad?

No movement came from his father's house. Just the porch light, burning steadily. There was no way his dad hadn't heard the gunfire. And if he heard it, he'd be doing something about it.

Unless he couldn't. Unless he'd been hit.

Another shot exploded. This time Mike could hear the bullet whistle above through the clump of bushes. Damn. That was close. Too close. They had to get out of here and find better cover, and they had to do it now.

He eyed the barnyard and area around the house. He needed something solid. Something they could hide behind that was more protective than a line of scraggly bushes. The squat concrete mass of the septic tank hulked between barnyard and house, only twenty feet from their hiding spot.

Perfect.

He grasped Cassie's arm and nodded at the

tank. *When I count to three, I want you to run for that tank, he mouthed.*

She nodded.

He released her arm. *Stay low.* He picked up his rifle.

Cassie did the same, moving her feet under her and tensing her muscles. He brought the rifle to his shoulder and trained the barrel slightly high, but in the area where the shots had originated. He couldn't see the shooter any longer, not a shadow, not a movement, and he didn't want to chance hitting one of his dad's horses in the pen beyond. He didn't have to hit anything, actually. He just needed to send the shooter ducking for a few moments.

Using his trigger hand, he held up his fingers, one at a time, counting to three. As soon as his third finger rose, he slipped his finger into place on the trigger and fired.

Cassie sprinted for the concrete tank and dove behind it.

Mike released a breath he wasn't aware he was holding. Thank God, Cassie had made it. She was safe, at least for now.

She scrambled to her knees and brought her rifle to her shoulder. She did exactly as

Mike had done, aiming the barrel high as not to hit anything she couldn't see.

He hadn't considered how he was going to get across the open span to the tank. But he should have known he could count on Cassie. He gathered his feet under him, ready to run.

She gave him a look and lifted her knee. She tapped it on the grass three times.

He pushed into a dead run, keeping as low as he could. A shot exploded from Cassie's rifle.

It seemed to take forever to cross the short distance. With each stride, Mike braced himself for the sound of gunfire, the sting of the bullet. He reached the tank, diving to the ground behind Cassie.

Mike's breath roared in his ears. Eyes on the shadows around the barn, he sucked in a breath and held it, struggling to hear over the thrumming of his heart.

The roar of an engine cut the stillness. Tires spun over gravel. A dark sedan raced from behind the barn and fishtailed onto the driveway. There was no way they could catch them, but Mike didn't care. He just wanted them out of there. Away from Cassie. He just wanted her to be safe. He didn't take a breath until the taillights disappeared over the ridge.

Cassie lowered her rifle. *Are they gone?*

I think so. But stay alert.

He and Cassie waited, wordless, for several moments. The night was silent except for the light rasp of their breathing, sending clouds of steam into the cold air. The moon lit the valley. Everything was so quiet, so peaceful, it felt like shots had never been fired, as if the past few tense minutes were a dream.

Something stirred in the shadow of the barn.

Cassie gasped. She held her fingers to her lips as if trying to keep the sound in.

Mike tensed, brought the rifle up. He strained to see through the dark shadow. He fought to hear the sound of movement, of anything.

A low moan reached him. The moan of a man.

The shadows moved again. Moonlight glinted off silver hair.

Mike's throat pinched. "Dad!"

CASSIE HANDED MIKE a foam cup filled with steaming coffee. The surgical waiting room of the hospital was vacant except for the two of them. No surprise. Only emergencies would send people to the surgery floor in the middle of the night. And while there were several people in the E.R. when they'd arrived, apparently only one needed surgery.

Mike's father.

Cassie met Mike's worried eyes. "Did you hear anything?"

Circles cupped under his eyes, nearly as dark as his fading bruises. He looked so tired. So worn down. "No. Not a word."

She ached to reassure him. To tell him his dad would be okay. But she didn't have any way of knowing if that would be the case. And she respected Mike too much to offer empty words. She sat down next to him on the stiff couch.

"If I lose him…"

She understood where his thoughts were leading without him finishing his sentence. It was a tragedy that Mike's father had been shot. It was a double tragedy that the last conversation Mike had with him was an argument. "If he's anything like you, he's strong. Strong enough to pull through."

"Why did I have to fight with him tonight? Why couldn't I have just kept my mouth shut and let him speak his piece?"

"This wasn't your fault. You can't beat yourself up over it. Your dad was the one who was critical of you. Your dad was the one who didn't support you, even though you did the right thing."

"You don't understand."

She remembered his words in his kitchen, before the gunfire had interrupted. There was more. More he hadn't wanted to tell her. "Then make me understand."

Elbows on knees, he cradled his head in his hands, his pain so sharp the air around him seemed to throb with it. "I had a brother."

Something shifted deep in Cassie's chest. She knew he had a brother. He'd mentioned Tommy before. His brother who'd been deaf since birth. That was why both he and his father were fluent in American Sign Language. And perhaps why Mike had never treated her deafness as a disability. But this time he'd said he *had* a brother. Past tense. As if he didn't have a brother anymore. She scooped in a breath. "What happened to your brother? Did he die?"

"I don't know."

She frowned. Had she read his lips right? "You don't know? What do you mean?"

"Tommy was younger than me, about seven years younger. Both my parents worked a lot and didn't have a lot of time to take us places. So whenever I went to a movie or anything, I'd have to bring Tommy along." He shook his head, the muscle in his jaw flexing. "I used to hate it when he tagged around with me."

"A lot of older siblings feel that way."

"You have brothers or sisters?"

She nodded. "Older brother. And I guarantee my brother thought I was a pest. For good reason, too. It's natural."

"Maybe. If resentment was as far as it went."

She swallowed, her throat growing tight. She couldn't imagine Mike doing anything to hurt anyone. He was a protector. She'd seen that firsthand. It was part of his nature as much as being a cop. A part that drove her crazy at times, but a good part all the same. "What happened?"

"I was seventeen and had a hot date." His lips twisted in a bitter smile. "Lisa Martinez. We went to a movie. I don't even remember what we saw."

She waited for him to go on, but his lips didn't move. He stared at the floor in front of him, as if sucked back to that day all those years ago. "And Tommy?" she prompted gently.

"Tommy had to go along. I didn't want to take him. I wanted to be alone with Lisa. All I thought about was being alone with Lisa."

"You sound like you were a typical teenage boy."

He shook off her words. "I gave him some money and told him to wait in the arcade until the movie was over. I left my deaf, ten-year-old brother all alone. No one to go to for help. Hell, people didn't even know sign language back then. Even if he'd tried to ask for help, no one would've understood him."

An empty feeling hollowed out in the middle of Cassie's chest. She knew what it would have been like for that little boy. People looking at him as if he was a freak. Or worse, turning their heads away, afraid to notice he was different, ashamed of their repulsion. Only she'd been nineteen when she'd lost her hearing. And she could speak. Tommy Lawson had neither of those advantages.

Her chest ached for Tommy, for Mike. Tears blurred, turning the hospital waiting room into a mosaic of lights and colors. She swiped at her eyes to keep tears from spilling down her cheeks.

Suddenly she didn't want to know what had happened to Tommy. It would be too painful, too close. She had only to look at the pinch of Mike's face to know. She had only to see the self-blame in his eyes.

"When the movie was over, Lisa and I walked over to the arcade."

Cassie sucked in a breath. As much as she didn't want to hear what came next, she knew Mike needed to tell her. Reaching out, she took his hand in hers, to give him comfort and to hold on for her own sake. "What happened?"

"I don't know. He was gone. No one admitted to seeing him. It was like he'd vanished."

"Did you call the police?"

"They tore the city apart. My dad was a cop, remember. Even then he was on his way up the ladder. A sergeant. The police did everything they could."

"They didn't find anything at all?"

"There were leads for a while. Things that got our hopes up. But none of them panned out. To this day, I don't know what happened to my little brother. But I do know whatever it was, it was my fault."

"Oh, Mike." She slipped her arm around him, pulling him close.

He stared straight ahead. Wooden. As if by accepting her hug, her feelings for him, he'd be betraying his brother. As if by taking even a moment's break from punishing himself, he would be letting Tommy down all over again.

"My father never forgave me. Not that he should. He's right. If I had taken care of Tommy, if I had done the right thing then, Tommy would still be here. Hell, my mom might be here, too."

"Your mom?"

"She died about five years after Tommy disappeared. Car accident."

"You can't blame yourself for that."

"I don't know. She didn't deal with the stress well. She was on medication. They said she fell asleep at the wheel."

There was more to that, too. More he wasn't saying. More that she could guess. "You think she died on purpose." She couldn't bring herself to say suicide. The whole thought was gut-wrenching. And to think that all these years Mike had lived not knowing about his brother, blaming himself, to have his mother commit suicide on top of it was just too much.

He shrugged a shoulder. "The insurance company tried to prove it was suicide, but they never could. Still, I don't know…"

Cassie shook her head. She needed to get through to him. She needed to help him. "You can't blame yourself for all of that."

He looked her straight in the eye. "Why not? Cassie, it was my fault."

"You were only seventeen."

"I knew better. I knew leaving Tommy alone was wrong. I just didn't care."

"You never thought anything bad would happen."

"No. But I should have done the right thing. My dad was right."

"Your dad was wrong to be so hard on you."

"And how was he supposed to be? He lost his son because of what I did. He probably lost his wife, too."

"You don't know that."

He shook his head. "I know enough."

She remembered what he'd said in the kitchen, before the bullets started flying. "That's why you insist on doing the right thing, isn't it? You're trying to make up for what happened?"

He shook his head. "I'm trying to prevent anything else from happening."

She wished it was possible to prevent tragedy and loss. But she had firsthand experience with that, too. "Sometimes you can't keep bad things from happening. No matter what you do. No matter how honest or responsible or deserving you are, they happen anyway."

He looked at her as if he'd just really noticed she was there. Really noticed who she was. "You lost your hearing, even though you didn't do anything to deserve it."

"Exactly. It just happened."

"And you're still angry."

"No. I was at first, but not anymore."

He looked back at the floor, as if he didn't quite buy her pronouncement but didn't want to call her on it.

"I just don't want to be treated differently because of it. I want to be like everyone else."

"But you're not like everyone else. You're extraordinary. You're the most extraordinary woman I've ever known."

His words warmed her chest and wound around her heart. She wanted to believe him.

She wanted to soak in his words and make them part of her. For so long, she'd battled insecurity. For so long she felt she had to struggle to be more, better, smarter. All to make up for what she'd lost. But it wasn't until right now, looking into Mike's eyes, that she felt she might have arrived. That she might not have to make up for anything anymore. "Thank you for that, Mike. It means a lot to me."

He twined his fingers with hers.

MIKE SAT for a long while, staring into Cassie's eyes, feeling her soft fingers between his, breathing in her scent. He didn't deserve her. He knew it, and he couldn't lie to himself. But neither could he release her hands. He needed her. To understand. To get him through this. To help him summon the strength he needed to face whatever he needed to face.

"Lawson, I just heard. Is he going to be okay?"

Mike tore his attention from Cassie to see Tim Grady standing in the doorway of the waiting room. "Grady."

Cassie pulled her hands from his and folded them in her lap.

"Sorry I interrupted." Grady stepped into the room. "Is he out of surgery yet?"

"No. I haven't heard anything." As sorry as Mike was that Grady had ended his moment with Cassie, he needed to talk to his former partner. He needed whatever help Grady could give him if he was going to get the bastard who had shot his dad. "Were you able to do those favors for me?"

"Sure was." Grady glanced at Cassie, as if reluctant to speak in front of her.

"It's okay. Cassie knows everything that's going on."

"All right." He flashed her a smile and lowered himself to the chair flanking the couch. "First off, Lois wants to go to The Palm."

Mike found a chuckle somewhere inside him regardless of all that had happened tonight. The Palm was one of the more expensive places in Denver, and he'd bet it was Grady who'd come up with the suggestion, not Lois. He knew Grady was still having trouble paying for all the medical expenses his wife's health insurance refused to cover. Grady probably hadn't been to a place like The Palm in a long while. "I guess it's the least I can do after cheating you out of your trip to the mountains."

"Damn straight. I haven't been able to use that cabin all year."

Mike nodded. He might not have many people willing to watch his back, but at least he had Grady and Cassie. "I hope Lois found something worth our sacrifice."

"Well, no."

"Nothing?"

"If you don't count Cassie's fingerprints in her own apartment, Lois found nothing readable."

Damn. So whoever had ransacked Cassie's apartment had been wearing gloves. That was one lead that turned out to be a dead end. Oh, well, it still would be worth paying for dinner at The Palm if the date with Lois helped Grady move on with his life. "Did you get the list of officers on the evening shift?"

"That, I can give you." He dug into his pocket, pulled out a square of paper and handed it to Mike. "I can't get a hold of the incident report yet, if one even exists. Not without drawing attention I'd rather not draw. I'll get it for you as soon as I can."

"Thanks, partner. This helps a lot." Mike unfolded the paper and deciphered Grady's sloppy hand. Davis, Marshall, Tutlen, Alvarez, Jacobs, Bruce. He stared at the list of officers who had been assigned to the downtown area last night. At least one of these officers had chosen to leave Cassie and him high and dry and facing a gunman. One of these officers was working for whoever wanted that disk. All he needed to do was find out which one.

Grady looked past him and focused on the waiting room's entrance. "News."

Mike pivoted on the couch, following his gaze.

A large man wearing blue scrubs walked toward them. Sweat glistened on his face, making his skin shine like black marble. "Michael Lawson?"

"Yes." He shot to his feet. "How's my father?"

"He's out of surgery and doing well."

"He's going to make it?"

"He's going to make it just fine."

A weight Mike hadn't fully recognized he'd been carrying lifted from his shoulders. His dad was going to be all right. They had more time. Time to talk. Time to work out their differences. Maybe even time to heal and move on.

Cassie stood beside him and reached for his hand.

He smiled down at her, then returned his focus to the doctor. "Can I see him?"

The doctor glanced at Detective Grady, then back to Mike. "I'm sorry. The police have insisted he speak with them first. I'm not sure when they'll clear you to visit. You'll have to discuss it with them."

The police. Of course. There had been a shooting. They would want to speak to the victim. "I understand. Is it the county sheriff?"

"Yes. And the Denver PD."

No wonder the doctor had glanced at Grady. Mike turned to his partner. "What's up, Tim? What aren't you telling me?"

Grady pressed his lips into a line. "It's not my idea, Mikey. I want you to know that. I'm arguing against the whole thing and I'll keep it up until the lieutenant comes to his senses."

Cold, hard tension balled in the pit of his stomach. "Why is the Denver PD in on this?"

"I'm sorry, man. But you're regarded as a suspect in your dad's shooting, too. We can't let you see him until we can clear you."

Chapter Thirteen

By the time Cassie called Evangeline and her boss sent PPS agent John Pinto to watch over Mike's dad, Cassie felt so rattled all she wanted to do was curl up in her bed and forget the past week had ever happened.

No, that wasn't true. She might want to forget all the crime and worry and danger, but she wanted to hold on to her time with Mike.

She watched him talk to John. The Native American agent was famous in the office for the meticulous way he planned every detail for each security job he worked. Cassie hoped his talent for thinking through all danger would put Mike at ease about his father's safety. She couldn't imagine anything more wrenching than the hell Mike had been through, and to be a suspect in the shooting, besides, seemed utterly cruel.

John paused, reaching the end of his litany of precautions and plans. "I'll take care of your father, Detective Lawson. Rest assured."

Mike let out a long sigh. "Thanks. I really appreciate it."

John nodded and turned to Cassie. "Evangeline wants to see the two of you at the office. A lot has happened since you left last night—and not just to the two of you."

Cassie almost groaned. They'd gone through the whole night without sleeping. She was still wearing her ugly gray sweats. Her joints ached and a headache had started behind her eyes. Not that she could sleep if she did get the opportunity. The way her mind was whirring, she probably couldn't sleep for the next week.

It didn't take long for her and Mike to reach the office. And from the moment they peered into the retina scanner and buzzed their way inside, Cassie could feel the energy bouncing off the office walls.

Evangeline spotted them through the glass walls of her office as soon as they made it past the spot where Angel was pouting behind the reception desk. Evangeline waved her hand. "Cassie, Mike, in the conference room. We were waiting for you to arrive. Angel, you, too, honey."

They filed into the conference room and took seats at the wide table. Jack Sanders, Sara Montgomery and Lenny were already there. Angel stood at the back of the room.

Evangeline walked in behind them and took her spot at the head of the table. She paused for a moment, looking at each agent in the room in turn. "Mr. Durgin is gone."

Cassie narrowed her eyes on her boss. She couldn't have read that right, could she? "Durgin's gone?"

"That's right."

Jack leaned back in his chair, as cool and in control as ever. "He decided he didn't want to stick around and enjoy our hospitality?"

Evangeline tilted her head to the side. "Apparently not. And he took the original of the disk with him."

Sara looked worried. Mike touched Cassie's arm.

Cassie shook her head. "It wasn't the only copy. I made several copies of the data."

Mike nodded and turned his attention back to Evangeline.

"Cassie's right. We lost nothing."

"Except our witness," Mike said. "How did he get out? It's not like you can just waltz out of this place unnoticed."

"It was my fault," Angel said, her eyes pooling with tears. "I let him out. He said he wanted to get some doughnuts."

All eyes in the room focused on the receptionist.

"He said he'd bring some back," she said, as if that made all the difference in the world.

Cassie felt terrible for the girl. Angel was a lousy receptionist, a disaster when it came to office equipment and a challenge to deal with even on her best days, but no one could doubt that her heart was in the right place. Cassie wished she could soothe the girl. Or at least scrape off some of the black makeup that was starting to run down her face.

As if reading Cassie's thoughts, Angel wiped her eyes with the side of her hand, smearing black back to her hairline.

Evangeline gave her a gentle smile. "I told you not to worry about it, Angel. I meant it. It's okay."

Angel nodded and stared at the floor, chomping her gum with even more of a vengeance than usual.

"How did he find the disk in the first place?" Mike asked. "Don't you have special security for such things?"

Evangeline nodded. "It would normally be locked away. But last night, I left the disk out on Cassie's desk."

Mike raised his brows. "You did? Why?"

"I wanted to see what Durgin would do."

"So you didn't trust him, either." Cassie smiled. She should have known Evangeline wasn't being as gullible as she seemed in letting Durgin stay at the PPS office last night.

Beside Cassie, Mike grinned, as well. "So now that we know Mr. Durgin is a liar and a thief, what happens now?"

"I asked Lenny to put one of his compact GPS devices into the disk's case."

Mike's smile widened. "So you're tracking Durgin."

Lenny nodded awkwardly. "That's right." He looked back down at the laptop computer he had on the table in front of him and adjusted the headset covering one ear.

Evangeline continued. "If he tried to take the disk—and I wasn't sure that he would— I wanted to find out what he'd do with it.

Durgin has a two-hour head start, but Ethan is tracking him as we speak. Lenny is in contact."

Cassie nodded. Although a bit of a loner, Ethan Moore was one of the most experienced agents at PPS. Tracking down Durgin should be easy for him.

"So you see, Angel, you did just what you were supposed to. You did a great job. After all, we aren't running a jail here. Durgin wasn't our prisoner. You did just what we needed you to do. Thank you." Evangeline gave Angel a reassuring smile.

Angel sniffed and ran her pierced tongue over her upper lip. "You're welcome."

Evangeline focused on Agent Sara Montgomery. Near Cassie's age, Sara looked a lot younger, yet she always seemed a lot older and more poised. At least in Cassie's eyes. "Sara?" Evangeline said. "What have you learned about the woman murdered last night? Lila Strotsky?"

"The FBI is aware of her. According to my source, she moved heroin for a 'big man' in the area. And she worked at a mob-run gambling club until about two weeks ago."

"How about her death?" Mike asked.

"My source says she was making noise about leaving the drug business and going straight. That's what they think got her killed. The FBI isn't convinced her death has anything to do with our situation."

Evangeline nodded. "All right. We'll keep looking into it. If there is even a slight possibility the Russian mob has something to do with these deaths, I want to know about it."

Mike glanced around the conference room. His gaze landed on Sara. "Where are the other agents who staked out Cassie's apartment last night?"

"They returned earlier this morning," Evangeline said curtly, answering for Sara. She turned to Jack. "What did you find out in your research on Kardascian's and Durgin's finances?"

Unease pricked at the back of Cassie's neck. Evangeline had changed the topic briskly. Too briskly, in her opinion. As if she was trying to brush over something.

"You're going to love this," Jack said. "After calling in favors at the Jefferson County Sheriff's Department and having a talk with Durgin's personal secretary, I found some interesting similarities. Both Kardascian and Durgin were facing a lot of personal debt. Both sold their companies to Tri Corp Media, taking shares in a blind trust run by the Kingston Investment Group as part of the cash buyout."

"Both of them?" Cassie said out loud.

Jack held up a hand. "That's not all. Remember Mitchell Caruthers?"

Cassie nodded. Caruthers was the personal assistant of movie star, Nick Warner. Caruthers had also stolen Warner's money and was responsible for his death. If it wasn't for Jack, Caruthers might have gotten away with it. "What about him?"

"He invested the money he stole from Warner in TCM stock."

Cassie nodded. She knew that part. They'd found out that detail shortly after Caruthers died. But knowing Jack, he'd saved the best for last. "And?"

"He also wrote a few large checks to this Kingston Investment Group."

"The blind trust," Mike said. He looked at Cassie. "So all three—Kardascian, Durgin and Caruthers—invested in this blind trust."

Cassie tried to get it straight in her mind.

"So is TCM the common link in all this or is it this Kingston Investment Group?"

"Hard to say. TCM has been swallowing up companies left and right recently. But that's not really unusual. They've made a lot of profit over the past few quarters. They need to reinvest."

"And Kingston?"

"I don't have any favors to call in there," Jack said. "And they're not eager to share. It's not going to be easy to get information about them."

"And there's always the possibility this investment group has mob ties," Mike added.

Sara nodded. "The Russian mob is moving into legitimate business areas like finance all across the country. It's the new trend the FBI is concerned about."

Evangeline frowned, lines digging into her forehead and deepening around her mouth.

"Evangeline," Lenny said.

Evangeline leaned toward Lenny, giving the computer genius her full attention.

"Ethan has located Durgin."

"Put him on speaker."

Lenny hit a few buttons.

"Evangeline?"

Mike translated Ethan's words into sign language so Cassie could follow the conversation.

"Yes, Ethan. You found Durgin?"

"Yes. But there's a problem."

"What is it?"

"He's dead."

Cassie felt the gasp rip from her throat.

"Do you have a cause?" Mike asked, then signed Ethan's answer.

"A call went out for an ambulance about ten minutes ago. The dispatcher said overdose. The ambulance is here now, but it's no longer in a hurry. Word is they lost him before it arrived."

Mike nodded. "Let me guess, heroin."

"Right."

Cassie folded her arms around herself. Another person dead. When was this going to stop?

"Thanks, Ethan. You might as well come back to the office and prepare for that fundraiser luncheon." Evangeline nodded for Lenny to cut the connection and turned her troubled eyes on Mike. "Detective Lawson?"

Mike nodded.

"I need to talk to you in my office. Right now."

He nodded and pushed back his chair.

Cassie pushed her chair back, as well. She was relieved that Evangeline had some sort of assignment for them. Sitting around worrying was the worst. At least now, she and Mike could do something. Look for answers. Work as a team. She rose from her chair.

Evangeline shook her head. "Not this time, Cassie. I need to talk to the detective alone."

MIKE ENTERED Evangeline's office, wariness gripping his nerves. He wasn't good at reading minds, but he was pretty sure that whatever it was she wanted to talk to him about, he wasn't going to like it.

Evangeline gestured to a chair near the glass wall that looked out onto the agents' cubicles. "Have a seat."

"I'd rather stand, thanks."

"I suppose you can guess why I asked to speak with you alone."

He could. The only time he'd been called on the carpet like this by a supervising officer, he'd learned of the police brutality complaint leveled by Kardascian. "You're terminating my assignment."

"Yes. I no longer need you to protect Cassie."

He opened his mouth, then closed it without speaking. He didn't trust his voice to come out sounding normal. He figured it would sound as strangled as his throat felt.

"I'd like you to help with the investigative side of this, if you'd like to continue at PPS. We need someone with your experience if we're going to track down whether or not this blind trust and its list of investors has anything to do with the Russian Mafiya."

That was fine. Investigation was his job. It was what he loved. But there was another concern that pressed against his chest like a physical force, making it hard to breathe. "What about Cassie?"

"I'm taking Cassie off the case."

"Why?"

"It's too dangerous."

"You knew it was dangerous when you asked her to decrypt that disk."

"I suspected. But I never thought it would go this far."

There was more. Evangeline knew something she wasn't sharing. "How far has it gone?"

She paced to the far side of her desk. Pulling her shoulders back, she turned back to face him. "Last night Cassie's apartment was set on fire. Lily barely made it out of there alive."

Something shifted inside his chest. He balled his hands into fists by his side. "Are Lily and Cameron all right?"

"They're fine. A little shaken, though. They both had some minor injuries that I insisted they have checked by a doctor."

"That's why they weren't in the briefing."

"It could have been much worse."

"Like if Cassie had been there."

Evangeline nodded. "Lily got out because she heard glass breaking in the loft just before the incendiary devices were tossed in. If it had been Cassie…" She let her sentence trail off.

Mike didn't need her to finish. He knew damn well what would have happened to Cassie if Evangeline had allowed her to bait the trap as she'd wanted. "How are you going to keep her safe?"

"I'm sending her to L.A. with Jack. If she's

not working on the disk anymore, there will be no reason to kill her."

As much as he hated the thought of being away from Cassie and of her losing the case she cared so much about, the only feeling he could manage at the moment was relief. The sooner she was out of this mess and safe in L.A., the better. "And you'll have Lenny finish the decryption?"

"It's mostly finished. We just have to figure out what the numbers mean."

Mike nodded. Easier said than done. Cassie still hadn't landed on an explanation that made that disk seem like anything but a jumble of numbers. But deciphering numbers wasn't going to be the tough part. "Cassie's not going to go along with this, you know."

Evangeline flinched, despite her usual cool. "I know. It's going to be hard."

"I'm not going to break the news. I'll take on whatever assignment you need me to do, but not that." He held up his hands. He knew he was being a coward. But that wasn't all of it. It wasn't the prospect of facing Cassie's anger that had him throwing up his hands. It was the fear of breaking her heart.

"You don't have to tell her. I will."

The door to the office flew open. Cassie stepped inside, her cheeks red, her nostrils flaring. "I'm not going to L.A. I'm staying to work on this disk. And if you refuse to let me do my job, then I quit."

Chapter Fourteen

"I'm sorry, Cassie. You're off the case. It's too dangerous."

"For a deaf girl?" Cassie blurted. Evangeline hadn't said the words, but she might as well have. Cassie had read every word she'd said to Mike through the glass office wall. And what it boiled down to was that Evangeline was yanking the most important case of Cassie's career out from under her because she was deaf.

"It's not just that."

Cassie held up a hand. "Save it. I'll send you my letter of resignation." She spun around and started out the door.

A hand gripped her arm. Mike.

She wrenched herself free. She couldn't talk to Mike right now. She couldn't stomach him trying to smooth things over. Not when she knew he wanted her off the case, as well. Not when he was probably happy about the idea of shipping her off to L.A.

She ducked out of the conference room without looking back. Making her way down the hall and past the agent cubicles, she slipped into the tech room.

Lenny looked up from his work. Embarrassment flushed his face, covering his freckles and contrasting with the orange of his hair.

So he knew. He knew Evangeline was reassigning the case to him before Cassie did. She supposed she shouldn't be surprised. Lenny knew everything that went on around here. Lenny was the one who made this office work. Still, the thought that he knew and obviously felt sorry for her made her humiliation complete.

She plunked down in her desk chair and started gathering her laptop, her BlackBerry and the personal photos she kept of her family. After the fire in her apartment, these few items might be the only personal property she owned.

The air currents shifted. The faint scent of leather teased her senses. Sucking in a breath of resolve, she turned to face Mike as he stepped beside her desk.

"Don't overreact to this."

Don't overreact? He had to be kidding. "Didn't you hear? Evangeline is yanking my case out from under me."

"Evangeline is worried about you. For good reason."

The air shifted again. Cassie glanced toward Lenny's workspace. Apparently he'd decided they needed a little privacy. That or his discomfort at the thought of taking over the most important case of her life had just gotten the best of him. Whatever the reason, she'd take it. She needed to vent and she'd rather no one at PPS witnessed it.

"Evangeline needs to let me do my job. If that job entails risks, it's up to me to decide whether I want to face them or not. She needs to give me assignments and let me do them, just like she does with Lenny and Cam and Sara and Jack and all the rest of people who work for PPS. I don't need her to coddle me. I need her to trust me to do my job. She has her projects. She doesn't need to make me one."

"Her projects?" Mike echoed.

"Like Angel."

He gave her a confused look.

"The receptionist. You know, black hair, multiple piercings. She has kind of a goth thing going on."

"Ah, yes. I know Angel." Mike nodded. "How is she Evangeline's project?"

"Evangeline likes to take in people. Give them a break, help them turn their lives around. I think it stems from her growing up in the foster-care system."

"That's admirable."

"It is. For people who need a break, Evangeline is a godsend. I just don't want her thinking the deaf girl is one of her projects. I can make my own breaks."

"Yes, you can. But in this case, someone is trying to kill you."

"And if Lenny takes over the disk decryption, someone will try to kill him. So why is Evangeline shipping me off and not Lenny?"

"I don't have an answer for that one."

"Yes, you do. Evangeline said it herself. I can't hear a window breaking. I'm deaf. And that means I'm less than other people. More in need of help. Of coddling. Well, damn it, I'm not less. I'm not less." Tears streamed down her cheeks, but she couldn't check their flow. She hated being this weak, this vulnerable. But she couldn't help it. She was too worn down to be strong. Too tired of death and danger. Too frightened and frustrated. A sob shook her chest and lodged in her throat.

Mike ran his fingers over her hair. Cupping his hand around the back of her neck, he pulled her toward him. He cradled her face against the crook of his neck and held her tight.

She could feel his voice rumble in his chest. And though she couldn't hear his words, his tone smoothed over her like a healing balm. Not patronizing. Not even particularly sympathetic. Just strong and steady and matter-of-fact.

What she needed him to be.

Swallowing into an aching throat, she pushed back from his shoulder and looked into his eyes. "Thank you."

"Don't mention it."

"Ever since I woke up that day in college, people have treated me like an invalid. My family. My friends."

"They were probably worried about you. I know Evangeline is."

"I know. I know they all want to protect me. They want me to be safe and happy." She shook her head. "But the hovering suffocates me. The endless concern…"

She blinked back the tears that had again started to fog her vision. She wasn't going to break down again. She wasn't going to let herself cry. She'd cried too much already. "It makes me feel that maybe they're right, you know? Maybe the world is too much for someone without hearing. Maybe I am less now that I'm deaf."

"If you're less now, you must have been a superwoman before."

She couldn't help but smile. "A supergirl."

"What?"

"A supergirl. There is no superwoman."

He gave her a smile, the corners of his dark eyes crinkling. "Maybe not in the comics. But the more I get to know you, the more I believe she's here in real life."

Cassie soaked in his smile, his touch, the look in his eyes. "Because she's deaf, her other powers are more developed?"

"Exactly."

"I hope so. Because now I'm unemployed." She'd meant the comment to be flip, a dry little joke, but it stuck in her throat and made her whole body ache.

"I'm sure Evangeline will give you your job back."

"If I agree to run off to Los Angeles, she will. But I'm not going to do that."

Mike nodded as if he wasn't surprised. "Let me guess, you're going to finish your work on that disk."

She dipped her hand into her pocket. Pulling it out, she held aloft a flash drive about the size of a business card but with a memory bigger than that of most computers. She leaned down and tapped the black case that held her equally powerful laptop computer. "I have everything I need."

Mike blew out a heavy breath. "Whoever is trying to kill you won't know you're no longer working for PPS. And they might not care even if they do."

"What are you saying? That I should run off to L.A.?" She hadn't realized it, but she'd been counting on Mike to back her up, to agree that her idea was the best course. The possibility that he agreed with Evangeline, even after she'd spilled her guts to him, stung.

"No. It might be selfishness on my part, but I want you to stay."

Cassie let out the breath she'd been holding. Her chest felt tight, not tense and aching, but like a muscle stretching. Mike wanting her in Colorado, especially for selfish reasons, meant more than she could say. Since that morning in college she'd dreamed of finding a man who would treat her as a partner. A man who wouldn't coddle her. A man who believed she was his equal. And though she was still afraid to hope, she had to admit she wanted that man to be Mike. "I guess I need to figure out where I'm going to stay."

"I have an idea. And since my original assignment with PPS is over, I might be in the market for something new."

"Or something old, like protecting me?"

"I have the feeling protecting you will never get old."

MIKE STEPPED OUT on the balcony overlooking what had to be one of the most rugged and beautiful former gold-mining gulches in the Colorado Rockies. He'd been to Tim Grady's cabin once before, a modest little log structure which, unlike Milo Kardascian's monstrosity, was made mostly of logs. But though he'd thought it was a beautiful setting for a card-playing retreat among a small group of cops, he hadn't remembered it being quite as breathtaking as he found it now.

Of course, that could be due to the improvement in company.

He unfolded the newspaper he'd picked up on the drive. Stepping away from the thin wooden rail separating him from the gulch below, he moved to the grouping of two outdoor chairs where Cassie sat frowning at the screen of her laptop computer. He didn't know how smart it had been to quit PPS and go off on their own. He'd insisted on certain precautions like Kevlar vests for the two of them. Still, there were a lot of variables. But he knew Cassie well enough to recognize she would have done it with or without him. And that more than anything, he wanted it to be with.

She glanced up at him, then nodded to the vacant chair. "I need some help brainstorming."

He refolded the paper and tossed it on the table positioned between the chairs. Reading the news could wait. "I don't know how much help I'll be, but I'll give it a shot."

"What types of numbers might you want to keep track of...and keep secret?"

"The bank account number idea didn't pan out?"

"I tried every way I could think of to organize the numbers the way account numbers would be organized, but it just didn't fit. I think it's something else."

"How about PIN numbers? Personal identification numbers for bank accounts."

She shook her head. "I tried that already. Unless the PIN numbers are of varying lengths, that's not it. I tried a combination of PIN numbers and account numbers, too. No good. I suppose it could be money amounts. But what purpose would that serve if the amounts weren't tied to anything else?"

Mike thrust to his feet. Maybe pacing would help him think. "Phones have numbers."

"Tried it."

"U.S. phone numbers and numbers abroad?"

"Check. What else?"

"Hmm." He walked to the end of the balcony, pivoted and headed back toward her. His footsteps beat out an even rhythm on the hand-hewn planks. "Addresses?"

She nodded. "Check. House numbers. Postal route numbers. Zip codes."

He continued with the geographical thinking. "Land coordinates."

"Land coordinates." Her eyes flared wide. "There would be numbers for longitude and latitude, right?"

"Right. Degrees, hours and minutes."

"And a North, South, East and West designation. Let me try." She tapped something into the computer.

He knelt down beside her chair, trying to make sense of what she was doing. It was no use. As far as he could see, she was just tapping gibberish into the keyboard. He lifted himself into his chair and snapped open the paper.

He'd read the entire front page, taken in a little more scenery and thought about what he'd throw together for dinner from the food they'd brought when Cassie let out a squeal.

She looked up from the screen, eyes sparkling. Reaching out, she gripped his hand in hers. "That's it. That's what's on the disk. Look." Her voice trilled with excitement, charging the air around them. She pointed down at the numbers.

"It looks the same as before."

"I reversed the process so I could show you what I did. You have to watch this."

He pushed the newspaper aside and knelt by her chair. "Okay. Let's see the show. I can't promise I'll understand it, though."

"Yesterday, I found the key that decrypted the numbers. Yet I couldn't figure out what the numbers meant, right?"

He nodded. At least he was with her so far.

"The numbers didn't make sense because the direction designations and signs for degrees, hours and minutes were still encrypted with a simple cipher. A cipher that turned them into numbers, just like the rest. But once I knew what I was looking for, I could figure out the cipher. And once I figured out that cipher…"

He leaned closer. The rows of numbers on the monitor shifted and changed. Suddenly each row of numbers was divided into degrees, hours and minutes. North latitude and West longitude designations appeared where numbers had been just moments before. "It's land coordinates, all right. A list of locations."

"Someplace with North latitude and West longitude could be in the United States."

He nodded. "I think a lot of these locations are in Colorado, if I remember my map coordinates from high school geography class."

"If we find out where these locations are, maybe we can figure out who sent the disk to PPS and how it fits into everything else that's going on."

"And why keeping these locations secret is worth killing for."

Cassie looked up at him, her face glowing with such excitement and accomplishment, he felt it tighten in the middle of his chest. "We did it, Mike."

No. Not we. "*You* did it, Cassie."

"I couldn't have done it without you." She shook her head. "Heck, I'd be dead right now."

He didn't want to think about that. He didn't want to think about anything but the sound of Cassie's voice, the glow in her eyes. Her, the moment, the setting—it all swirled around him like a fog. Exciting, penetrating, overwhelming. "Lord, you're beautiful."

She dipped her chin, looking down at the laptop.

He shouldn't have said it, he knew. But somehow he couldn't stop himself. He didn't want to stop himself. He brushed his fingertips along her jawline and tilted her face back up. "Cassie, I…"

"Just kiss me," she said, her voice barely above a whisper. Her lips parted, waiting for him, beckoning him.

Cupping her face with his hand, he brought his mouth to hers. She tasted warm and sweet and impossibly arousing. He deepened the kiss, twining his tongue with hers, taking her in and locking her in his heart. He could never get enough of this, of her. Certainly not from a mere kiss. And when the kiss ended, it was far too soon.

Cassie pulled back slightly and watched him. Her gaze melted into his, her face so full of longing and strength and beauty, he almost couldn't breathe.

He leaned toward her. Right now he didn't care about land coordinates or encrypted disks or mysterious blind trusts. Right now all he could think about was kissing her, touching her, holding her body tight to his and never letting her go.

"So what are we going to do?"

"Right now?" He had a million ideas. All of them centered around kissing her again…then taking off her clothes.

"We have to tell Evangeline."

He let out a breath and sat back on his haunches. She was right. This wasn't over. And as much as he wanted to give in to the want pulsing through his body, he had to keep his head together. At least for a little while longer. "We'll call her."

"No. I can use my BlackBerry. I can send her the coordinates right away."

He managed to keep his distance while she tapped all the information into her little handheld device. When she finally finished and set her BlackBerry on the table, his arousal had hardened into an uncomfortable ache. "It's kind of cold out here. Do you want to go inside? Celebrate?"

She smiled, soft, seductive. "What do you have in mind?"

He hadn't even been aware of moving until his lips found hers. He lifted her to her feet and pulled her tight to him. He'd wanted her so much, for so long, now that she was in his arms, he couldn't stop himself. He couldn't think. All he could do was feel.

He took her lips. Slipping his tongue into her mouth, he twined with hers, danced with hers. He moved his hands over her back, down the delicate line of her spine. Reaching her buttocks, he cupped her and pulled her against him, molding her body to his.

Perfect fit.

He buried his other hand in her curls, holding the back of her head as he teased her lips with his, as he plundered her mouth.

She moaned deep in her throat, the sound both trembling in the air and quaking in her chest. And his.

He moved his mouth along her jawline and down her neck.

She leaned her head back into his hand, trusting him to hold her, baring her throat. Her scent swirled around him, fresh like the mountain spring, but warm. So warm.

He littered kisses over her collarbone. Slipping his hand down from her hair, he smoothed her sweater over her shoulder, taking her bra strap with it.

She had beautiful shoulders. Smooth and

redhead pale. Freckles lightly dotted the tops of her arms. He kissed each one, wanting more of her, wanting all of her.

Her hands skimmed over his shoulders and worked their way between their chests.

Mike pulled back a few inches, just enough to watch her fingers work.

She unfastened the Kevlar vest and unbuttoned her soft sweater, letting both hang open to expose the lacy bra beneath. Her hands moved to the bra's center clasp. She unhooked it and spread the cups wide.

Her breasts were as pale and creamy as the rest of her. Her pink nipples tightened.

He sucked in a breath. He pushed the vest, sweater and bra off her shoulders, letting them fall to the deck. He sat on the edge of one of the chairs and pulled her close until she was standing between his open thighs. Her breasts just below eye level, he skimmed his hands up her sides and cupped their fullness. He circled a nipple with his tongue and teased the nub with his lips, his teeth.

She arched her back. And he took her nipple fully into his mouth, suckling and teasing until she cried out.

He moved to the other breast, teasing and sucking, breathing in her scent. He moved his hands down her ribs, over the curve of her waist and swell of her hips. Finding the waist-band of her jeans, he made quick work of button and fly and pushed them down her legs, taking her panties with them.

He rubbed his hands up her thighs. Slipping his fingers between her legs, he lightly touched her folds, her warmth, her wetness.

She moaned and thrust her hands into his hair. Stepping out of her jeans, she spread her legs, exposing herself to him, allowing him inside.

He caressed and teased, moving his fingers against her harder, faster, bringing her to the brink.

She moved her body against the pressure. Her legs began to shake.

Mike pulled his hand out from between her legs and held her tight against him, propping her up.

She groaned. "Don't stop."

"I wouldn't dream of it." He pushed himself up from his chair and guided her into it. Reclin-ing the back, he pulled her hips to the chair edge and knelt down. He eased her thighs open and moved between them.

He brought his mouth to her, kissing her most intimate place. She tasted clean and sweet. He wanted more. He wanted all she had to give.

She relaxed her legs, trusting him implicitly, opening to him. She breathed deep, releasing each breath with a whispered moan.

He swirled his tongue over her.

A shudder rippled through her body. Once again, she ran her fingertips over his scalp and held on to his hair.

He deepened the contact, tasting her with his whole mouth. He moved his hands up her body, cupping her breasts as he slipped his tongue inside.

Another shudder seized her. She arched her back, moving against his mouth, holding on to him as if she'd never let him go. She threw her head back, calling out his name, releasing her tension in shudder after shudder.

When her climax had stilled, he kissed and caressed his way back up her body. Her skin was slick despite the cold. But as the night fell, she would become chilled.

When he reached her lips, he kissed her deeply.

"That was amazing," she mumbled against his lips.

"You're amazing."

She smiled, soft, vulnerable. "You make me feel amazing. The way you look at me. The way you kiss me. I feel like a super-woman."

"Supergirl."

A low and sexy laugh bubbled deep in her throat. "Now let me make you feel all power-ful."

"You've already done that. And besides, I'm not finished yet."

He rose to his feet. Gathering her into his arms, he lifted her from the chair. She was a small woman, but she felt lighter than he thought possible. Light, delicate and so soft.

She circled her arms around his neck. "You have a plan, I see."

"Yes, I do. Leave everything to me."

"I'm all yours."

He carried her across the balcony to the cabin's door. He would take her inside, curl up with her in a warm bed. Take care of her. Love her.

Love her.

He didn't know why he hadn't realized it before now, but there it was. Somewhere along the way his feelings had grown and deepened until they filled every thought in his head, every heartbeat, every breath.

He loved Cassie Allen.

He loved her smarts and toughness. He loved the sweet vulnerability she showed no one but him. He loved the way she opened to him…trusted him…relied on him.

And more than ever, he had to make sure he never let her down.

MOONLIGHT FELL through the window, sparking off Cassie's hair and turning it to glowing fire. She curled on her side, cuddling the oversized pillow under her head, her curls fanned out all around her.

Mike brushed a strand back from her cheek. They'd made love for hours, tender and fierce. Cassie had been unlike any woman he'd ever known. Trusting him, moving with him. So open and intimate, it was as if she'd shared not only her body, but her heart, mind and soul, as well.

And now she slept, trusting him to watch over her, to keep her safe.

Fatigue drilled deep into Mike's bones, but he couldn't sleep. His mind raced. Thoughts of Cassie, worries about her safety, the feeling he was missing something, all of it twisted and tangled in him until he just had to move. He pushed up from the bed. Careful not to disturb her, he pulled on his clothing, threw on his vest to keep himself warm and stepped out to the balcony.

The night had grown cold in the hours they'd been snuggled warm in bed, fresh with a snap of snow in the air. He took in breath after breath, willing it to clear his mind. Cassie might have figured out what was on that disk, but he had a feeling this was far from over.

He thought of Cassie, of what had happened between them, of what he suddenly knew had been there since they'd first met. He thought he'd been worried about her safety before. Now the fear of losing her clamped on to his nerves like a terrier refusing to let go. It was as if his love for her was a precious gift he didn't deserve. And he couldn't shake the feeling that no matter what he did, he was bound to lose her. And worse, he was bound to let her down in the process.

He flipped open the newspaper he'd picked up on the way to the cabin. If he didn't quit obsessing about losing Cassie and start doing something to prevent it, he was going to drive himself crazy. If it was up to him, they'd leave the cabin and both fly to L.A. or Hawaii or anywhere else tonight. But since it was unlikely flights would be leaving in the dead of night and Cassie hadn't slept for two days, he'd have to hold off until morning. He flipped to the paper's local page and focused on the newsprint. If he was lucky, there might be something about Lila Strotsky's death or the investigation into Kardascian's murder.

He flipped to the local page and scanned articles ranging from failed tax-reform policies to a dispute over the profitability of converting oil shale to usable fuel. Nothing on Kardascian. He scanned the rest of the section. On the second page, his gaze landed on an article about a gang fight in a downtown nightclub that had claimed three lives. The paper interviewed an officer he'd worked with before he made detective. An officer by the name of Kale. The last time he knew, Kale had been promoted to the day shift. How had he found himself back on evenings?

Mike's gut hitched. Evenings? He checked the date of the incident. The gang fight had taken place the night before last. About two hours after the break-in at Cassie's apartment. Two hours after the shooter in the dark sedan had tried to kill her.

The roar of his own heartbeat pulsed in his ears. He dipped a hand in his jeans pocket and pulled out the folded paper Grady had given him. The names of the officers on the evening shift that night. The officers who would have been covering the downtown area. Davis, Marshall, Tutlen, Alvarez, Jacobs and Bruce.

Kale's name wasn't among them.

Mike took a deep breath. Then another. It wasn't possible. Grady must have made a mistake. He must have missed Kale's name in the lineup. He must have—

Something slammed into his side, just below his left shoulder. The force threw him against the balcony rail. Wood cracked and splintered under his weight. The railing gave way, leaving nothing between him and the treetops below. He fell. Crashing through tree branches. Hitting ground. The report of the gunshot echoed off rock as he rolled down the gulch's steep slope.

Chapter Fifteen

A hand grabbed Cassie's shoulder. Mike? She moaned and snuggled deeper into her pillow. She didn't want to wake up. She didn't want the wonderful, warm sensations coursing through her bloodstream and snuggling close to her heart to end. She wanted him to crawl back into bed, spoon his body around her and fold back into sleep.

The grip hardened. Fingers pressed into her flesh with bruising force.

A jolt of alarm shot through her. She pushed away her dreams and opened her eyes.

The cabin's bedroom was dark, only illuminated by stripes of moonlight peeping between the wooden slats of window blinds. But even in the dim and streaked light she could recognize the man standing at the foot of the bed.

Mike's partner, Detective Tim Grady.

Confusion and panic fogged her mind. "What's going on? Where's Mike?"

Two other men stood in the room, as well. One formed a dark, solid, hulking silhouette behind Grady. The other knelt on the edge of the bed, pale and smaller, but judging from the corded muscle standing out on the arm gripping her shoulder, he didn't have to be big to be strong. He yanked her up to a sitting position in the bed.

She grasped at the bedcovers puddled around her waist and pulled them over her naked breasts. "What are you doing?"

Grady stared at her with hard eyes. Since she'd met the man, she'd rarely seen him not smiling. He wasn't smiling now. He switched on a dim floor lamp at the base of the bed, just bright enough to reveal the movement of his lips. "Where's the damn disk?"

Her mind scrambled for an answer. "It was stolen…from PPS. James Dur—"

"I know you made a copy. Where is it?"

Of course he knew. Mike had explained everything when he'd asked to use Grady's cabin. Details shuffled into place in her mind.

"You killed him, didn't you? You killed Durgin? And Kardascian, too."

His expression didn't change and he didn't bother to deny the charges. "If you want your clothes, answer."

"And Lila Strotsky, too?"

"No. Not Strotsky." He bit off the words, as if it angered him that she would believe he'd killed someone he hadn't.

So he had killed the others. She thought about how Grady had appeared so concerned after Mike's father was shot. "How about Mike's dad?"

Behind Grady, the behemoth shifted his bulk from one foot to the other. "That wasn't supposed to happen. He looked just like Mike."

"Shut up," Grady barked over his shoulder. He focused dispassionate eyes back on Cassie. "Where's the copy?"

She glanced around the dark room. The flash drive was still in the laptop. Where had she left the laptop?

"Pull her out of the bed."

The wiry man's hand tightened. He started to pull.

She scrambled to hold on. "Wait."

He paused, his hard eyes digging into her.

She'd sent the coordinates to Evangeline. And PPS had other copies of the disk. What did it matter if they got hold of her laptop? "It's in my laptop. It's on a flash drive."

"Where's the laptop?"

Cassie tried to think. Mike had brought the laptop, her BlackBerry and her clothes inside after they'd made love the first time, while she'd waited for him to return to bed. "It's in the cabin. I'm not sure where."

Grady waved a hand to the man on the bed. "Stevens, go look."

Focusing a disappointed look at the spot where the sheet covered her chest, he thrust himself off the bed and left the bedroom.

A shiver shot up Cassie's spine. Stevens. One of the Dirty Three. She'd guess the hulking silhouette behind Grady was another of the corrupt cops. So where was the third? And where was Mike?

She had to think fast. They could take the flash drive if they wanted it, but she had to figure out a way to get them to leave Mike and her unhurt. "PPS is sending some agents. They're on their way right now."

"Really?" Grady's expression didn't change. His face wasn't angry, wasn't alarmed, wasn't anything. It was just...dead. Void of any feeling whatsoever. "I find it hard to believe you'd be waiting for PPS agents to arrive by lying around naked in bed. Unless they aren't coming here on business."

The hulk behind him chuckled. He shifted his weight. Light from the window reflected off a dark shaved scalp.

"Mike was supposed to wake me up... before they arrived."

"Lawson won't be doing any waking anymore, that's for sure," the cop behind Grady said.

A muscle twitched in Grady's cheek. "Shut up, Fisher."

Her chest squeezed. Something had happened to Mike, then. Something bad. A sob worked its way up her throat. She choked it back. She had to stay calm. She had to think. If there was a way she could get away from them and find Mike, maybe she could help him. Maybe things weren't as dire as Fisher wanted her to believe. Maybe Mike was still alive.

He had to be still alive.

She had to think of something...fast. "I already deciphered the disk."

Grady's features seemed to darken. "What was on it?"

Her heart lodged in her throat, beating hard enough to make her choke. "I don't understand. Don't you know what's on the disk? Weren't you trying to kill me to keep me from finding out?"

"We were paid to keep you from finding out," Fisher blurted. "But that doesn't mean they told—"

Grady held up a hand, cutting him off.

Cassie's mind raced. So they didn't know. They'd just been paid to stop her, to kill her. Paid by whom? The Russian mob, as Mike had worried? Or someone else? Someone Grady was hoping to double cross or blackmail with the contents of the disk? "Who are you working for?"

"You really think I'd tell you?" Grady raised his arms to shoulder height. He held a pistol in his fist. "What was on the disk, Cassie?"

She struggled to breathe. She'd played this wrong. All wrong. She didn't know what to do, what to say. If she told him, he wouldn't need to keep her alive. But if she didn't, would he shoot her? Would he kill her right now? Just as he'd killed Mike?

No.

She forced herself to draw air into her lungs. One breath after another. She couldn't accept that Mike was dead. She wouldn't. He had to be alive. "Let Mike and me go, and I'll tell you what was on the disk."

The wiry cop who had grabbed her shoulder walked back into the room. "Found it." He lifted up the black case that held her laptop.

Grady smiled, but instead of the gap between his teeth making the gesture endearing, it gave him a malevolence that stole Cassie's breath. "Guess I don't need to ask you. Guess I can just look it up myself." He holstered his gun and snatched the laptop from Stevens. Laying it on the foot of the bed, he unzipped the case.

Behind him, the hulk raised his weapon, keeping her in his sights in case she tried anything.

Another cop stepped into the room behind Stevens. The third member of the Dirty Three, no doubt.

Grady glanced at him as he opened the

laptop and turned it on. "Rodriguez, you find his body?"

Blood pounded in Cassie's head. His lips had formed the words "his body." She was sure of it. Oh, God, was Mike really dead?

"He went through the railing when you shot him. Looks like he rolled down the incline and into the gulch." Rodriguez shook his head. "No way he survived that fall. Not with a bullet in him."

A trill of hope rippled up Cassie's spine. He hadn't found Mike's body. He didn't know for certain that Mike was dead. She grasped that thought and held on. There was still a chance, a chance both she and Mike could get out of this. "I wasn't lying about PPS agents coming. They're probably on their way right now."

Grady ignored her, all his attention on the computer's screen. The glow of Cassie's Rocky Mountain wallpaper reflected blue on his face.

"Evangeline promised they'd be here by daybreak."

"Shut up," Fisher said, twitching the gun as if to remind her he held it.

Grady looked up from the computer. "What's your password?"

Her password. Of course. He couldn't access the files in her computer without it. She still had the upper hand. "I'll give it to you only if you leave Mike and me here."

"Mike Lawson is dead. You heard Rodriguez."

"Then you shouldn't mind leaving him."

Grady shook his head. "Maybe not. But do you really think we're planning to let you live?"

A cold lump balled in the pit of her stomach. No. She didn't. They'd tried to kill her before. Now that she could identify the four of them, they'd kill her for sure. But still, she had to try. She had no alternative. "I won't tell anyone about any of this. I know how to keep my mouth shut."

Fisher's big shoulders moved in a laugh and Rodriguez joined in.

Cassie held on to the panic whooshing in her ears and bubbling under her skin. She couldn't let it break free and carry her away. She had to think. "You're going to have to believe me if you want the password."

"Don't be ridiculous."

"The agents are on their way." She nodded to the window, to where the slightest yellow glow rimmed the ridge to the East. "It'll be dawn soon."

"No one is coming for you, Cassie. You know it and I know it."

She swallowed into a dry throat.

"But I'd be an idiot to kill you in my own cabin. I have another place in mind. A place where no one will ever find your body."

She shivered, giving in to the tremor claiming her. So this was it, then. They had probably killed Mike and now they were going to kill her. "You're too late. It's all over. I already sent the deciphered data to Evangeline."

Grady looked up from the computer, his brows low. "Then a couple of us will just have to pay a visit to Evangeline this morning. I'm sure our employer won't mind if Evangeline Prescott disappears. Now get out of that bed."

Cassie gripped the sheet. There was no way she was standing up naked in front of these men. If she was going to die anyway, she had nothing to lose. "Go to hell."

"Get her up," Grady said to Rodriguez and Stevens.

The men closed in on her. Stevens grasped the blankets, ready to rip them off her body.

Cassie set her chin. They might strip her naked. They might kill her. But that didn't mean she had to give them what they wanted. "Wait. I'll tell you. Just let me get dressed."

Grady grinned and held up a hand, signaling the dirty cops to stop their assault. "Fine. What's the password?"

"Rachmaninoff."

He shook his head. "The composer? You've got to be kidding. You really are a brainiac, aren't you?"

"Throw me my clothes."

Stevens picked up her jeans and sweater from the place Mike had stacked them when he'd cleared their things off the deck. "Would you look at this?" He held up Mike's belt, the holstered pistol attached. He slipped the belt over his shoulder and tossed Cassie's clothing on the floor far enough from the bed that she'd have to slip out from under the sheets to retrieve them.

Bastard.

Taking a deep breath, she threw back the covers and climbed out. Cold air intensified her shiver. She could feel the creeps' eyes all over her. She struggled into the clothes as quickly as she could, forgetting about bra and underwear.

At the foot of the bed, Grady typed in the password. He hit the enter key. "What the hell?"

Cassie couldn't keep the spiteful smile from her lips. "Oh, I'm sorry. Instead of the password that opens the files, I must have given you the one that encrypts the whole system. How silly of me."

Grady made it around the bed in two seconds flat. Reaching her, he drew back his arm and plowed his fist into her jaw.

Cassie's head snapped back. Her head rang. Her vision narrowed, swimming with darkness. She sagged against the edge of the bed, then slumped to the floor. She needed to warn Evangeline, but she didn't know how. She couldn't even stand...or think. Copper filled her mouth. Blood oozed sticky and hot from her split lip and chin.

Through her fog she could feel Fisher, Stevens and Rodriguez surround her. Their hands grabbed and lifted her. Then the prick of a needle stung her arm and the world went totally dark.

MIKE THOUGHT he'd heard somewhere that death was quiet, peaceful and pain-free. But judging from the agony screaming through his body, he'd been horribly misled.

He tried to lift his head and get a look at the rock outcropping where he'd finally landed. The dark skeletons of aspen just starting to leaf out clung to the side of the mountain all around him. He lay on his side. A clump of trunks protruded behind his back, no doubt responsible both for stopping his descent and the ache in his spine. He had no idea how long he'd been here. At some point in his tumble, he'd blacked out. And try as he might, he couldn't see the cabin in the darkness.

No, not the darkness. The first glow of dawn.

The gentle blue light that preceded sunrise lit the slope and reflected off the light snow that had fallen overnight. Trees surrounded him, etched shadows against the snow and masses of rock.

So time had passed. But not too much.

The events before his fall jumbled in his aching head. The force of something hitting him. The crack of wood as the railing gave. The report of a gun.

He was still alive thanks only to the Kevlar vest he'd slipped on. The vest he'd decided to wear only because he was cold.

He was even colder now, but at least he was alive. And whoever had shot him was up there at the cabin.

Whoever had shot him? Hell, he knew who'd shot him. He'd known since he read that article in the paper about Officer Kale. The same person who had tried to kill Cassie and then covered his tracks. The same person who had shot his dad, then shown up at the hospital offering sympathy. The same person Mike had gone to for help and shared detail after detail about the case.

His partner.

Anger kindled inside him, growing until it burned hot. Anger and desperation.

Up in the cabin, Cassie curled in bed, unable to hear the gunshot. Unable to hear an intruder.

Fear gripped his chest. Adrenaline spiked his blood. He had to reach Cassie, before it was too late. She'd brought him so far. Given him his life back. She was relying on him. And God help him, he wasn't going to let her down.

He leaned forward, rolling from his side to his chest, then levering himself up onto his forearms. His head spun. His stomach retched.

He breathed slowly, getting hold of his nausea, willing his balance to return.

He must have hit his head in the fall. Likely he had a concussion. But that didn't matter. Nothing mattered except Cassie. Except saving her. Being there for her.

Not letting her down.

He gritted his teeth and pushed himself to hands and knees. Rock bit into a cut on one of his shins. Pain washed through him, bringing back the nausea.

He pushed on. Putting one hand and knee in front of the other, he moved up the steep slope. Slowly. Too slowly. The sky pinked, washing the mountain with a warm glow, though the air was so frigid he could see his breath.

But the frigid air and dusting of snow no longer kept him cool. Pain and exertion heated his body like a furnace. Sweat trickled down his back and chest and stung his eyes.

He reached the edge of the rock outcropping and moved onto an expanse of grass and gritty dirt. Trees clustered, their roots finding purchase in the soil. He negotiated around clumps of brush and located an area of softer dirt, vegetation washed away and soil eroding from rains and melting snowcaps from above. His fingers slid into an indentation. He looked down at a squat footprint, an oversized cross between dog and cat.

Mountain lion prints.

He shivered, trying to move faster. He sure as hell hoped he didn't run into the originator of those tracks. His gun was in the bedroom where Cassie slept. And though the animal wasn't likely to attack a man under normal circumstances, it would be able to sense that he was injured. Hell, it would be able to smell his blood from the cuts and scrapes that he felt covering his body. If it was hungry enough or had young nearby, he would be hard-pressed to protect himself.

He kept crawling, moving up through the washed-out area. His heart pounded with the stress. His lungs ached. But eventually he could see a dark shape behind the trees on the ridge above.

The cabin.

But he hadn't made it. Not yet. The slope up to the cabin's balcony was the steepest, and from where he crawled, it seemed to reach straight up into the sky.

Grabbing the trunk of an evergreen, he

pulled himself to his feet. A wave of dizziness washed over him. He fought it back. If he wanted to reach Cassie in time, he had to move faster than he could on hands and knees. He had to be able to stand, to pull himself up that slope.

He moved from tree to tree, pulling himself up on the trunks. He was still moving too slowly. The sun had peaked over the horizon and was now climbing in the sky. His only hope was that somehow she'd awakened. That she'd gotten to safety. That she'd found a hiding spot.

Or that she'd picked up his gun and shot the bastard.

He reached the logs bracing the balcony. Stopping at the base of the stairs, he strained to hear over his own heartbeat and the morning songs of birds.

No voices. No movement.

He moved slowly up the stairs, waiting for another bullet to come screaming out of the forest at any moment. Waiting for the force of the impact to send him sprawling back down the mountain.

He made it to the balcony. Flattening himself against the log wall, he inched along the outside of the cabin until he reached the door.

Gathering himself, he gripped the knob and pushed inside.

Again, he waited for a bullet. A sound. Anything. Again, nothing happened, nothing moved. He strode for the bedroom. The place where he'd last seen Cassie. The place where he'd left her curled in peaceful sleep.

He pushed open the bedroom door. He focused on the rumpled bed.

Empty.

His chest seized. He scanned the room, looking for any sign of what had happened, anything that might tell him where Cassie had gone. His belt was gone from where he'd draped it on the back of the chair. The gun holstered to it gone, as well.

The second time he'd lost his gun this week.

The Kevlar he'd brought for Cassie was gone, too. And her clothing. He could only hope she'd awakened. That she'd figured out something bad was going down and had slipped out before Grady had found her.

Grady and, no doubt, the Dirty Three.

He combed the empty room, his gaze freezing on a spot near the bed. Something dark stained the plank floor. His throat grew thick. Despair drilled into his chest. He bent down, head spinning, and touched the spot. His fingers came away sticky. He held them to his nose and inhaled the copper scent of blood.

Chapter Sixteen

Cassie came out of the sedative they'd given her with a fuzzy head and the dank scent of the grave permeating her senses. Although she knew her eyes were open, darkness surrounded her completely. She lay on something hard. Rock, most likely. And walls rose steep on either side, as if she'd been buried alive.

Oh, God, where was she?

Steel handcuffs bound her wrists behind her back. She lay tilted to one side, the press of her weight making her arms numb with lack of blood flow. She tried to lift her feet, to see how high the ceiling of her prison was above her head, but her legs were shackled, too. She settled for lifting both as high as she could. Almost numb from cold and lack of circulation, her feet scraped a ceiling of rock that seemed to angle to a point.

She could crouch in this small space. That was bigger than any grave she'd heard of. And that also meant there was air. At least more than she'd find in a buried pine box.

So where was she?

Judging from the dank smell, the rock walls and the size of the space, she'd guess one of the abandoned gold mines in the area. Just as good as a grave. Only instead of suffocating, she'd die slowly of dehydration.

The glow of a flashlight shifted toward her. Its beam bounced through the narrow burrow and illuminated the rough rock walls. Shadows long and short writhed as the light drew closer.

The light hit her face, blinding her. She shut her eyes and braced herself for whatever happened next.

Moment stretched after moment. Finally, she opened her eyes.

Grady crouched in front of her, focusing down at something in his hands. If he'd spoken to her, she'd missed it. Not that it mattered. He could ask from now until Christmas and she wouldn't give him the key to decrypt her computer contents. Not since she was certain he'd kill her anyway. Even if he promised to leave Evangeline alone at this point, she wouldn't believe him. But there was something she wanted to ask him. Something she really needed to know. "How could you do this?"

He glanced to the side, his hands still on whatever it was he was fiddling with. She could see the movement of his lips in the flashlight's glow. "Money."

"I mean how could you do it to Mike? You're his partner. You're supposed to back him up, not—" Her throat tightened.

"Kill him?" Grady shook his head. "I didn't want to. I knew his association with your company would bring him into this case the moment Evangeline Prescott needed a cop at her beck and call. So I tried to head it off."

"Head it off? How?"

"I arranged it so he would lose his gun and be suspended."

"But his gun…you used it to shoot Kardascian."

"Blame yourself for that one. You and Evangeline. Mikey was out of the picture until you two sucked him back in. If you hadn't hired him on at PPS, he never would have had anything to do with this. Deputy Chief Lawson wouldn't have been shot and Mikey would still be alive."

Her throat constricted. Her chest ached. Here Mike had been so worried that he'd endangered her, yet it had been the other way around. She'd endangered him.

Some backup she'd turned out to be.

"You know, that's the real reason I'm going to kill you. You made me turn on my own partner. You made me kill a man I've admired my whole career." He stood, half-crouched to avoid hitting his head on the mine's low and uneven ceiling. "So think about that when this little device goes off and the rock is falling in around you. If it weren't for you, Mike Lawson would still be alive."

A sob worked its way into Cassie's throat, choking her. Was he right? Was it partly her fault?

She watched Grady and his flashlight disappear up the sloped and uneven floor of the mine shaft, leaving her in darkness, leaving her to die.

She didn't want to die.

She didn't know where the voice came from inside her, but she knew she had to listen. She'd never given up. Not her entire life. And she couldn't let herself give up now.

Tensing stomach muscles toughened by pilates and yoga, she jackknifed her body into a sitting position. Stretching her arms as long as she could and bending her back, she slid her butt through the circle of her arms. The handcuffs bit into her wrists, awakening her numbed arms and making them scream with pain. She wiggled her weight from one hip to another, easing her hips through, following with her legs, until her arms were bound in front of her instead of behind.

She wasn't going to die stuck in a mine shaft. Not if she had anything to say about it. And although she had no earthly idea how she'd get out of this situation, she'd think of something. She had to.

She just hoped this brilliant plan presented itself before she was buried alive.

EVEN FOR AN AMATEUR like Mike, the tracks in the fresh snow were easy to follow. He moved as quickly as he could, using part of the broken deck rail as a walking stick. But as hard as he pushed, he knew it wasn't fast enough.

He found Grady's Jeep parked off the road, about a mile from the cabin. According to the tracks, they'd split up at the Jeep. Two likely getting into another car and two continuing past and winding back into the mountains. The tracks moved along the ridge before descending down a less steep slope to another ridge below.

If it was someone besides Grady leading this expedition, Mike would have almost thought they'd lost their way, wandered into nowhere. But Grady hunted this area. He knew it better than he'd known the rough neighborhoods in Denver when they'd worked together on patrol. He was heading somewhere, all right.

The question was, where?

And could Mike make it all the way there?

He gritted his teeth, willing his legs to keep moving, his mind to ignore the sharp pain that ripped through his side with each heavy breath.

Over the next rocky outcropping, he spotted a structure protruding from the side of the next slope. Ancient and weathered, the wood that made up the sloppily built shack appeared to be a hundred years old and ready to blow over in a stiff wind.

An abandoned gold mine.

He didn't have to walk a step farther to see that the tracks he was following led straight to the structure's entrance.

A bad feeling shifted into his gut. Abandoned mines like this from the Colorado gold-rush days dotted this region of the mountains. Every so often, the newspapers would contain stories of careless explorers falling down fifty-foot stone shafts and getting crushed in cave-ins. Tragedies. But tragedies that were witnessed. The victims' loved ones knew what had happened, even if the reality was horrible indeed.

If Grady had his way, Cassie would never be found. Once the light coating of snow melted, there would be no sign that they'd ever been here.

Mike could only pray he wasn't too late. That Grady and the Dirty Three hadn't already dropped Cassie down a deep shaft or caved in a tunnel. That she wasn't already dead.

Chapter Seventeen

Mike heard the click of a lighter flicking to life. The scent of cigarette smoke drifted to him on the light breeze. He flattened himself to the side of the structure just as Kurt Stevens emerged from the abandoned mine.

Glancing around the valley, the wiry cop took a drag off his cancer stick as if this was any other day, any other circumstance—as if he wasn't conspiring to commit another murder.

Mike's pulse pounded in his ears. The thought that a cop, any cop, could murder innocent people turned his stomach. No, it made him mad. Damn mad. And somehow, regardless of the "brotherhood of blue" and all that other bull, he doubted any cop would have a problem with what he was going to do now.

Hell, after all this, Stevens, Fisher, Rodriguez and Grady didn't deserve to call themselves cops. They deserved to call themselves inmates.

He grasped a good-sized board from the spot where it lay near the structure's entrance. He'd only have one shot at this. In the shape he was in, if he missed, Stevens could disarm him with little problem. It would all be over for him and for Cassie.

If it wasn't already.

He blocked that possibility from his mind. He had to focus. He had to make this work.

Hands shaking, he lifted the board, holding it like a baseball bat, ready to hit it out of the park. Pain shot down his side, making it hard to breathe. He gulped in air and held it. He stepped behind Stevens. He swung.

The dirty cop whirled around. He raised a forearm, blocking the blow. Wood cracked. Bone cracked. A bellow broke from Stevens's lips.

No time to think, Mike released the board. He showed his right hand under Stevens's raised arm and jabbed his fingers into the man's eyes.

The bellow turned into a scream. Stevens clawed at his hand.

Mike's legs wobbled. His ribs were on fire. He had to find a way to put Stevens out. Now. If he didn't end this quickly, Stevens would. Mike countered with a punch to the gut.

Stevens doubled over.

Bringing his knee up, Mike connected with his skull.

His head snapped back. He sagged to the ground.

Mike followed with a kick to the head, and Stevens went still.

Scooping a breath into his aching lungs, Mike grabbed the pair of handcuffs Stevens had on his belt. Dragging the compact but damn heavy man to a nearby aspen, he circled Stevens's arms around the trunk and secured his wrists. That done, he pulled the dirty cop's weapon from his belt, checked to see that it was loaded and headed back to the structure's entrance.

Where were the others? Judging from the tracks, two had driven away. That left one. The only one who knew the area well enough to find his way to this mine.

Grady.

Mike crept back to the structure's gaping doorway. The sun was now climbing in the morning sky, melting snow and streaming in stripes through the gaps in the wood. He focused on the dark hole in the side of the mountain…the gold mine itself.

His heart slammed against his ribs, shooting pain through his side with each beat. He was tired, too tired. His vision was starting to swim. Pain and injuries were taking their toll. Sweat stung his eyes and made Stevens's pistol's grip slick as ice in his hand, even though the air was cool.

He couldn't stop now. He had to keep going. He had to find Cassie before it was too late.

He walked to the mouth of the tunnel. The opening was small and irregular, likely cut and blasted into the mountains over a hundred years ago when the gold had already been panned from the streams and miners started burrowing into rock to find their fortunes.

Damn, but it was dark. The blackness was impenetrable. He needed a flashlight. There had to be one somewhere. Stevens couldn't have negotiated these tunnels without one. He must have set it down when he lit up.

Mike turned around. Hand on the wall of the tunnel, he stepped back toward the entrance.

A footfall sounded behind him. A barrel pressed against his temple. "So you didn't die, after all."

Mike's stomach hollowed out. "What the hell are you doing, Grady?"

"Holding a gun to your head and ordering you to drop yours. So drop it."

Mike opened his hands. The gun slipped out and clattered on the rock. "I mean this. All this. What are you doing killing people? You're a cop, damn it. Doesn't that mean anything to you?"

"Wake up, Mike. Those days of idealism and public service, they're over."

He couldn't believe Grady was saying this. Grady. The man who'd been as idealistic as Mike back when they were patrolling the streets. No, more idealistic. "That's what the job is about. Protecting citizens. Upholding the law."

"Really?" Grady's voice was hard as the rock around them. "And when those citizens and their politicians cut our pay to the bone so they can have a little tax break, we're just supposed to take it? And when they start whittling away at health care for us and our families? Are we still supposed to put our necks on the line and cheerfully pay those hospital bills ourselves?"

He knew where this was coming from. Janey. The runaround Grady had gotten from insurance companies unwilling to pay for experimental drugs that might have saved her life. The bills he was left with after her death. But even though his gripes were legitimate, they didn't come anywhere close to justifying what he had done, the path he'd chosen to follow. "This isn't the way to change things."

"I've given up on changing things. I get it now. This is the new way, Mikey. Survival of the fittest. Everyone has to take care of his own. No one is going to do it for you. Not even the Denver PD."

"So who did you sell out to? The Russian mob? Who?"

"I sell my services to the highest bidder. Whoever is most willing and able to pay. The taxpayers are too busy looking out for themselves to pay for law enforcement? Fine. Any smart cop will start looking out for himself, too."

"Any dirty cop." Mike grimaced from the taste of bile crawling up his throat at Grady's warped view of the world.

"We enforce the law. We can decide what's dirty and what's just smart business."

"When is killing smart business, Grady? When is killing anything but murder?"

Grady's fist jabbed Mike hard in the kidney.

Mike choked back the groan pressing at the back of his throat. His eyes watered. He had to find a way to escape Grady. But how? After the beating his body had taken, he didn't have the strength to overpower a man who lifted weights every morning of his life. A man who happened to be holding a gun. He had to find a way to distract him. And until he did, he needed to keep him talking. "So how are you planning to murder me, partner?"

"Believe me, Mikey. I didn't want to kill you at all. I wanted to keep you out of this. But now that you're in it, I can't see you just walking away."

Damn straight. Mike would never walk

away. He had to do the right thing. Not just because he'd promised Tommy. He had to do the right thing for himself. "What have you done with Cassie?"

"Funny you should ask. I was just setting Ms. Allen up to disappear. There's room for two." He prodded Mike in the back. "Walk."

Mike's legs wobbled under him. He stumbled, hitting his head on the rough-hewn ceiling.

"A little tired, Mikey? Climbing out of the gulch wear you out?" He stepped down the tunnel from Mike and pulled him to his feet. "I have to admit, you're one tough bastard. I always liked that about you."

A shadow loomed behind Grady. Before Mike could make out what it was, it slammed into Grady's back, knocking him forward into Mike.

Mike's knees hit rock. He braced himself on Grady, preventing a headlong sprawl.

Grady twisted, shining the flashlight on his attacker.

Spotlighted in the beam, Cassie raised her bound hands. Gripping the small rock, she attacked again.

Grady threw up his hands, blocking her

second blow. The flashlight fell, its shaft of light bouncing crazily around the rock walls. Something else clattered to the ground. Grady's gun?

Mike groped the floor with his hands. He had to find that gun.

His fingers touched nothing but rough rock.

Next to him, Grady started to rise. He pushed up, shoving Cassie back, sending her stumbling into the darkness.

To hell with the gun. Mike launched himself at Grady. He hugged his legs, tackling him.

Grady fell forward. Catching himself with his hands, he kicked back.

A boot plowed into Mike's face. Pain jolted through his neck and echoed along his nerves.

Grady kicked again.

Mike's head snapped back. His thoughts swam. He couldn't black out. He had to pull it together. Knowing he couldn't take another hit, he released Grady's legs.

His partner climbed to his feet, backing into an offshoot of the main tunnel, nothing but gaping black shadow behind him. The flashlight rolled along the floor, coming to a rest at the far wall. Its light illuminated Grady's face from below, making his lowered brows and gap-toothed grimace look like a kid telling a slumber-party horror story. But he was no kid. And this was certainly no story. He started to raise his hand, his pistol in his fist.

Mike launched himself. He plowed into Grady's legs.

His partner stumbled backward into the shadows. Suddenly he was falling, screaming. The gun fired. Its earsplitting report echoed through the tunnel.

Deep within the mine, an answering explosion sounded.

Cassie scrambled to her feet. She grasped Mike's arm, pulling him up. "We have to get out of here! Grady! He set explosives!"

Explosives. To seal off the mine. To bury Cassie alive.

Mike grabbed Cassie's bound hands. Half-leaning on each other, they ran. Behind, rumbles joined with the original blast, gaining in volume, chasing them. Clouds of dust overtook them. Feet slipping on loose rock, they pushed their legs as fast as they could go.

They emerged from the structure as the

boards started to go. Lumber rained down, accompanied by rock from the slope above the entrance. Mike grabbed Cassie's hand and ran with everything left in him. They emerged from the structure as the wooden wall beside them collapsed.

Just beyond the last wood wall, Mike's legs gave out. He went down on his knees, Cassie beside him. For a few moments, they remained there, waiting for the next rumble, the next shift. Afraid to move.

A crash shook the structure as another part of the tunnels underground gave way. "It's still unstable. Let's get away from here." Mike's legs wobbled with fatigue. He stumbled.

Cassie slipped under his arm, propping him up.

"The Jeep. It's up that ridge." He tried to lift his other arm. Halfway up, his muscles gave out and he let it fall to his side.

"Okay. Let's go."

"I don't know if I can make it, but you can. You can bring back help."

"I'm not leaving you."

"You have to. It's the only chance. For both of us. Let me down here."

She did as he said, dropping to her knees

in order to lower him to the ground gently. But instead of continuing in the direction of the Jeep, she turned back to the mine.

"Go," he urged.

"I have a better idea." She scrambled to her feet and started back toward the mine.

"Cassie."

She kept walking, not able to hear him. For the first time he noticed the cuffs on her legs, a steel loop attached to each ankle, the chain between smashed.

As she drew close to the half-caved-in structure, a rock slid down from the slope above.

Mike's chest seized. The explosion might have made the rock formations up the slope unstable. Even the wooden building itself still had pieces balancing precariously on one another, large pieces that could fall.

"Cassie, stop! It's too dangerous!"

She kept walking, oblivious to his shouts. She reached the spot where Stevens was cuffed to a tree. Bending down, she picked something out of his coat.

She carried it back to where Mike was sitting. As she drew close, he could see she held her BlackBerry. Hands still bound, she tapped at the little keyboard.

Mike let out a relieved breath, making his chest ache twice as hard. "You called for help?"

She nodded. "I asked Evangeline to send a helicopter and warned her the other two are on their way."

"You're something."

Cassie smiled, but something about her expression was more sad than happy or relieved. Tears shone in her eyes.

"What is it?"

She waved his question away. "Don't talk. It might take a while for the helicopter to get here. You need to save your strength."

"Then you'd better tell me what is bothering you."

She peered back in the direction of the mine. "I asked Evangeline to call for a rescue crew. For Grady."

"Good." If anyone deserved to die, it was probably his partner. But Mike still couldn't stomach the idea any more than he could stomach what Grady had become. "He might be still alive. Sometimes there are pockets in the shafts that don't cave in with the rest. People have been known to come out of something like this unhurt."

He studied her face. She still wasn't telling him everything. "That's not all."

She pressed her lips together.

"You can tell me. Whatever it is."

She looked down at the ground. When she returned her gaze to his face, tears tracked down her cheeks, making streaks in the thick dust. "He said I was responsible. That if you hadn't taken the assignment protecting me, you wouldn't have been drawn into this mess. You wouldn't have been shot. You wouldn't have almost died."

"He was rationalizing what he did. You didn't buy into that crap."

She dropped her gaze, then looked back up when he touched her arm.

"Did you?"

"I wanted to give up. When I heard him say it was my fault, I really wanted to die right then."

"But you didn't. You kept fighting. You got out of there." Gritting his teeth, he reached a hand to her face, touching rock dust over smooth, smooth skin. "I'm the one who let you down, Cassie."

"You let me down? How?"

He blew out a derisive breath. "I was on

my knees. Literally. If you hadn't jumped Grady with that rock when you did, it would have been over for both of us. I couldn't do it alone."

"Oh, God, Mike. You don't have to always do everything alone. You don't always have to be strong and take all the responsibility. That's what backup is for."

Chills fanned over his body that had nothing to do with the cool air. She was right. He hadn't seen it until now, but he didn't have to do everything alone. He never had with Cassie. She'd helped him and been there for him. And he wanted to always be there for her. "I love you, Cassie. More than you could ever know."

"I love you, too." She leaned down and kissed him on the forehead, probably the only place she could find that wasn't scraped or bruised. "You're going to be okay, you know."

"I will be. Thanks to you." He wasn't referring just to his physical injuries. It was more than that. Far more. "I'm grateful you and Evangeline walked into my hospital room that morning. Just the thought of how low I was makes me want to take you in my arms and never let you go."

"That sounds good to me."

He could see the love shining in her eyes. Strong. Unconditional. And deeper than any gold mine. "I'm a lucky…" He grimaced as a sharp pain seized his side. Damn broken ribs.

Her eyes widened in alarm. "Shh. Save your strength." Tears and dust streaked down her face. Her lip and jaw were swollen and starting to purple. And through it all, she looked more beautiful than ever.

He forced his lips to curl into something he hoped resembled a reassuring smile. "Don't worry. I'll get through this. With you backing me up, I can get through anything."

Epilogue

Cassie stopped at the door to Mike's hospital room reluctant to interrupt the visitor inside. She wished she could hear what they were saying without having to see their lips. But whatever the conversation was about, good energy emanated from the room. Quiet. Peaceful.

Mike's father spun his wheelchair around to face her. He gave her a smile, the lines fanning out from the corners of his eyes making him look warm and friendly. "What? No rifle?"

She laughed and tried to ignore the pain in her lip and chin at the sudden movement. "They wouldn't let me bring it past security."

"I heard you don't need guns anyway. I heard you can save the day with your bare hands."

Raising her bandaged hands and wrists, she crooked a brow. "Rocks. Rocks help."

"However you did it, thanks."

"Don't thank me. It was Mike who climbed up the mountain and tracked me down. And it was Mike who got us out of there in one piece." She peered past the father and focused on the son, her heart doing a little hop.

Four broken ribs, a broken nose and multiple lacerations and bruises later, he still looked pretty darn good. Angel wouldn't be able to control herself.

Former Deputy Chief Lawson pressed his lips together and nodded. "He done good."

In the bed beyond his dad's chair, Mike pressed his lips together, as well.

Cassie's throat tightened. It was so good to see father and son working their way back to each other. It might take a while to heal twenty years' worth of wounds, but the process had begun.

"Did he tell you his lieutenant was here?"

She looked to Mike, trying to figure out what a visit from his lieutenant could mean. "Really?"

"Mike was cleared of any negligence, as far as losing his weapon is concerned. His suspension is lifted. And he's getting commendations for bringing down Tim Grady and the other three and for saving your life."

"That's wonderful." Cassie beamed at Mike. It was about time the Denver PD gave Mike the reward he deserved. Maybe it would start a new chapter in Mike's life. One where the people who mattered most would appreciate him. Support him. Love him. She sure was ready to do her part.

"I'll leave you two alone."

Cassie started. She'd been so caught up in Mike, she'd nearly forgotten his dad was still there. She shook her head. "You don't have to do that. I didn't mean to interrupt. I can wait."

"Nah. If I don't get back to my room, that busybody nurse is going to come looking for me." He slowly wheeled his way out. At the door, he paused and peered up at Cassie. "Treat him good, would you? He deserves it."

"I sure will." Cassie walked to Mike's bed. "He's right, you know. You deserve happiness."

He shook his head, though his smile made his face look lighter than she'd ever seen it. "I'm convinced that sometimes good things happen. Whether you deserve them or not. Just the way bad things do."

She nodded. He might have something there. "Maybe it all evens out. Eventually."

"Maybe. But I don't want to question my luck too much. I just want to enjoy it. Every second that we have together."

"I couldn't agree more." Here they both looked like they'd been through hell—they had—and yet she'd never been happier.

"Did they find him?"

Grady. Cassie didn't want to talk about him. The whole thing was so tragic. So misguided. So wrong. "They recovered his body. They're not sure if he died in the original fall or if the mine's collapse killed him, but whichever it was, he's gone."

Mike nodded. "I'm sorry any of it had to happen in the first place. How about the Dirty Three?"

"The agents of PPS headed off Fisher and Rodriguez. They and Stevens are being held at the county jail."

"Has anyone been able to question them about who they were working for? Or did they lawyer up?"

"Ethan, Jack and Evangeline had a chat with

Fisher and Rodriguez before the authorities arrived, but they said Grady was the only one who had contact with their employer. Evangeline thinks they're telling the truth."

"So it's a dead end."

"We have the land coordinates. Lenny's working on identifying and plotting all the locations. If we find out the importance of those locations, maybe we can figure out who is behind all this."

He gave her a smile—sexy despite the bruises and bandages. "Maybe. I'm glad they're handling it. All I want to focus on is you." He cupped his hand around the nape of her neck. Raising his torso from the bed, he tried to bring his lips to hers.

He sucked in a sharp breath.

Cassie put one of her bandaged hands on his chest, pushing him back to the bed. "What are you thinking? You have broken ribs. You have to heal."

"Kissing you heals me."

"I mean it. Recover. Then you can kiss me all you like." She shot him a teasing smile. "And I need you to do much more than that."

"I thought at one point you said you didn't need anybody."

"I don't need someone to coddle me. But I would like someone to make me happy. And I have a whole list of things I need you to do to make me happy."

"Sounds like a very special assignment."

"It is."

"What exactly would it entail?"

"Long hours."

"I'm used to that."

"Fierce dedication."

He tapped his chest, covering his wince of pain with a grin. "That's me. Most dedicated man on the force."

"I thought you were the most honest man on the force."

"That, too."

"Good enough. But there's one more thing. The most important thing of all. This assignment requires you to believe you deserve as much happiness as you give me."

"Okay. I give in. From now on, we'll suck up all the happiness we deserve and more."

"Tommy would want that. Your dad wants it, too."

"I know. So where can I sign up?"

Warmth swelled in her chest until she felt

like the most special woman in the world. "Right here." She tapped her lips with a finger and leaned down to him.

* * * * *

Next month, the investigation and PPS's assignment intensifies when Elle James's book, COWBOY SANCTUARY, becomes the next installment in BODYGUARDS UNLIMITED, DENVER, COLORADO

Dante Raintree stood with his arms crossed as he watched the woman on the monitor. The image was in black and white to better show details; color distracted the brain. He focused on her hands, watching every move she made, but what struck him most was how uncommonly *still* she was. She didn't fidget or play with her chips, or look around at the other players. She peeked once at her down card, then didn't touch it again, signaling for another hit by tapping a fingernail on the table. Just because she didn't seem to be paying attention to the other players, though, didn't mean she was as unaware as she seemed.

"What's her name?" Dante asked.

"Lorna Clay," replied his chief of security, Al Rayburn.

"At first I thought she was counting, but she doesn't pay enough attention."

"She's paying attention, all right," Dante

murmured. "You just don't see her doing it."
A card counter had to remember every card
played. Supposedly counting cards was impossible with the number of decks used by
the casinos, but there were those rare indi-
viduals who could calculate the odds even
with multiple decks.

"I thought that, too," said Al. "But look at
this piece of tape coming up. Someone she
knows comes up to her and speaks, she looks
around and starts chatting, completely misses
the play of the people to her left—and doesn't
look around even when the deal comes back
to her, just taps that finger. And damn if she
didn't win. Again."

Dante watched the tape, rewound it,
watched it again. Then he watched it a third
time. There had to be something he was
missing, because he couldn't pick out a single
giveaway.

"If she's cheating," Al said with something
like respect, "she's the best I've ever seen."

"What does your gut say?"

Al scratched the side of his jaw, consider-
ing. Finally, he said, "If she isn't cheating,
she's the luckiest person walking. She wins.
Week in, week out, she wins. Never a huge

amount, but I ran the numbers and she's into us for about five grand a week. Hell, boss, on her way out of the casino she'll stop by a slot machine, feed a dollar in and walk away with at least fifty. It's never the same machine, either. I've had her watched, I've had her followed, I've even looked for the same faces in the casino every time she's in here, and I can't find a common denominator."

"Is she here now?"

"She came in about a half hour ago. She's playing blackjack, as usual."

"Bring her to my office," Dante said, making a swift decision. "Don't make a scene."

"Got it," said Al, turning on his heel and leaving the security center.

Dante left, too, going up to his office. His face was calm. Normally he would leave it to Al to deal with a cheater, but he was curious. How was she doing it? There were a lot of bad cheaters, a few good ones, and every so often one would come along who was the stuff of which legends were made: the cheater who didn't get caught, even when people were alert and the camera was on him—or, in this case, her.

It was possible to simply be lucky, as most

people understood luck. Chance could turn a habitual loser into a big-time winner. Casinos, in fact, thrived on that hope. But luck itself wasn't habitual, and he knew that what passed for luck was often something else: cheating. And there was the other kind of luck, the kind he himself possessed, but it depended not on chance but on who and what he was. He knew it was an innate power and not Dame Fortune's erratic smile. Since power like his was rare, the odds made it likely the woman he'd been watching was merely a very clever cheat.

Her skill could provide her with a very good living, he thought, doing some swift calculations in his head. Five grand a week equaled $260,000 a year, and that was just from his casino. She probably hit them all, careful to keep the numbers relatively low so she stayed under the radar.

He wondered how long she'd been taking him, how long she'd been winning a little here, a little there, before Al noticed.

The curtains were open on the wall-to-wall window in his office, giving the impression, when one first opened the door, of stepping out onto a covered balcony. The glazed window faced west, so he could catch the sunsets. The sun was low now, the sky painted in purple and gold. At his home in the mountains, most of the windows faced east, affording him views of the sunrise. Something in him needed both the greeting and the goodbye of the sun. He'd always been drawn to sunlight, maybe because fire was his element to call, to control.

He checked his internal time: four minutes until sundown. Without checking the sunrise tables every day, he knew exactly when the sun would slide behind the mountains. He didn't own an alarm clock. He didn't need one. He was so acutely attuned to the sun's position that he had only to check within himself to know the time. As for waking at a particular time, he was one of those people who could tell himself to wake at a certain time, and he did. That talent had nothing to do with being Raintree, so he didn't have to hide it; a lot of perfectly ordinary people had the same ability.

He had other talents and abilities, however, that did require careful shielding. The long days of summer instilled in him an almost sexual high, when he could feel contained power buzzing just beneath his skin. He had to be doubly careful not to cause candles to leap into flame just by his presence, or to start wildfires with a glance in the dry-as-tinder brush. He loved Reno; he didn't want to burn it down. He just felt so damn *alive* with all the sunshine pouring down that he wanted to let the energy pour through him instead of holding it inside.

This must be how his brother Gideon felt while pulling lightning, all that hot power searing through his muscles, his veins. They had this in common, the connection with raw power. All the members of the far-flung Raintree clan had some power, some heightened ability, but only members of the royal family could channel and control the earth's natural energies.

Dante wasn't just of the royal family, he was the Dranir, the leader of the entire clan. "Dranir" was synonymous with king, but the position he held wasn't ceremonial, it was one of sheer power. He was the oldest son of the previous Dranir, but he would have been passed over for the position if he hadn't also inherited the power to hold it.

Behind him came Al's distinctive knock on

the door. The outer office was empty, Dante's secretary having gone home hours before. "Come in," he called, not turning from his view of the sunset.

The door opened, and Al said, "Mr. Raintree, this is Lorna Clay."

Dante turned and looked at the woman, all his senses on alert. The first thing he noticed was the vibrant color of her hair, a rich, dark red that encompassed a multitude of shades from copper to burgundy. The warm amber light danced along the iridescent strands, and he felt a hard tug of sheer lust in his gut. Looking at her hair was almost like looking at fire, and he had the same reaction.

The second thing he noticed was that she was spitting mad.

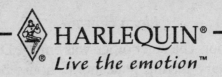

Harlequin® Historical
Historical Romantic Adventure!

Imagine a time of chivalrous knights and unconventional ladies, roguish rakes and impetuous heiresses, rugged cowboys and spirited frontierswomen— these rich and vivid tales will capture your imagination!

Harlequin Historical . . . they're too good to miss!

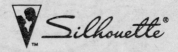

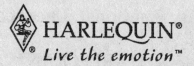

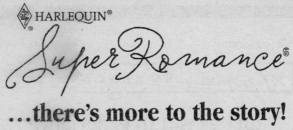
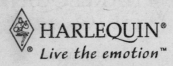